* * * * * *

"What's going on, Mr. McKenna?"

"Oh, hi, Mary. It seems we have a Peeping Tom in the neighborhood."

"Did you see who it was?"

"No. I didn't get a good look at him. It's too dark. He sure took off in a hurry when I yelled at him, though," he said with a slight chuckle in his voice.

"You might want to keep your windows locked and your drapes closed at night," he suggested.

"I'll do that, and thank you for running him off."

Mr. McKenna just smiled, waved and then went on his way. Mary closed and locked the window, then closed the drapes. She felt uneasy knowing that someone had been watching her. It sent a cold chill down her spine. She couldn't understand why anyone would be interested in her and what she was doing. She tried to put the uneasy feeling aside, but it was difficult for her.

* * * * * *

Other titles by J.E. Terrall

Western Short Stories
The Old West
The Frontier
Untamed Land
Tales from the Territory

Western Novels
Conflict in Elkhorn Valley
Lazy A Ranch (A Modern Western)
The Story of Joshua Higgins

Romance Novels
Balboa Rendezvous
Sing for Me
Return to Me
Forever Yours

Mystery/Suspense/Thriller
I Can See Clearly
The Return Home
The Inheritance

Nick McCord Mysteries
Vol – 1 Murder at Gill's Point
Vol – 2 Death of a Flower
Vol – 3 A Dead Man's Treasure
Vol – 4 Blackjack, A Game to Die For
Vol – 5 Death on the Lakes
Vol – 6 Secrets Can Get You Killed

Peter Blackstone Mysteries
Murder in the Foothills
Murder on the Crystal Blue
Murder of My Love

Frank Tidsdale Mysteries
Death by Design
Death by Assassination

THE RETURN HOME

by
J.E. Terrall

ISBN: 978-0-9963951-1-3

Printed in the United States of America
First Printing / 1996 – www.lulu.com
Second Printing / 2015 – www.creatspace.com

Cover Photo: The Thompson Building in Depot Town Historic District of Ypsilanti, Michigan, taken by J.E. Terrall

Book layout/
Formatting: J.E. Terrall
Custer, South Dakota

[illegible]

Check Out
[illegible] The [illegible]
Book
[illegible]
Cost: $12.0[illegible]
Due date: 11/1[illegible]

[illegible]
Book
[illegible]
Cost: $1[illegible]
Due date: 11/16/2015

[illegible] Murder [illegible]
[illegible]
Book
[illegible]
Cost: [illegible]
Due date: [illegible]

[illegible]
Book
Sullivan, James
Cost: $2[illegible].00
Due date: 11/16/20[illegible]

[illegible]
Book
Sullivan, [illegible]
Cost: $[illegible]
Due date: 11/16/2015

[illegible] PM

Library Information

Huron Public Library

Receipt for Patron 25958000387316
Patron Report Class: Adult

<u>Today's Transactions</u>

Check Out
35958002378261 The Return Home
Book
Terrall, J. E.
Cost: $12.00
Due date: 11/16/2019

35958002375911 Murder in the Foothills
Book
Terrall, J. E.
Cost: $12.00
Due date: 11/16/2019

35958002378576 Murder at Gill's Point
Book
Terrall, J. E.
Cost: $12.00
Due date: 11/16/2019

35958001826393 24: Deadline
Book
Swallow, James,
Cost: $25.00
Due date: 11/16/2019

35958002183372 Midnight at the Bright Ideas Bookstore
Book
Sullivan, Matthew,
Cost: $26.00
Due date: 11/16/2019

10/22/2019 01:52:23PM

library.huronsd.com

THE RETURN HOME

This book is dedicated to my loving wife, for
without her love and understanding, her
encouragement and support, this
book most likely would not have
been written. Thank you.

CHAPTER ONE

MARY WESTON LEANED BACK in the seat of the Boeing 747 as it flew high above the clouds. She was returning to her hometown of Ypsilanti, Michigan, after almost twenty years of working at a mission school in the mountains of Peru. It would be several hours before the plane would land at the Detroit Metro Airport, about thirty miles from her hometown.

She closed her eyes and tried to nap as her thoughts turned to the reason for her return. She had received a letter from Arthur Hopkins, an attorney, notifying her of her grandmother's death and that everything had been left to her. She had been thinking about returning home for a long time, the letter simply provided a reason to do it now. It had taken several weeks for the letter to find her at the remote mountain school, and another couple of weeks for her to arrange for a flight back to Michigan.

Mary dozed off and on during the long flight. A change in the sound of the jet engines woke her from one of her few moments of rest. She could hear the jet engines reduce speed as the plane started the long slow descent to the airport. A tone sounded when the "No Smoking" and "Fasten Your Seat Belt" signs lit up. She could feel the vibrations in the plane as the landing gear dropped down into position. Suddenly, there was a slight jar as the big plane touched down on the runway. The engines roared as the pilot slowed the plane for the taxi to the terminal.

As soon as the plane rolled to a stop, Mary stood up and stretched. She gathered her bags from the overhead compartment. Mary slowly worked her way to the front of the plane and out onto the long ramp leading into the terminal.

As the crowd of people getting off the plane disappeared into the terminal, a gray-haired man approached her. She had to look twice, but she was sure it was Mr. Hopkins.

"Mary Weston?" the man asked politely.

"Mr. Hopkins?"

"Yes. How was your flight?" he asked as he reached out to help her with her carry-on bags.

"Long would be the best way to describe it," she replied.

"I'm sorry about your grandmother."

"Thank you."

"I have a car waiting near the luggage claim area. Will you be staying, or will you be returning to Peru?" he asked as they walked through the terminal.

"I'll be staying. Other than that, I haven't made any plans yet."

"I understand. I hope you don't mind, but I had my cleaning lady go over to your grandmother's house and do a little cleaning so that you could stay there if you wish."

"Thank you very much. I would like to stay there. I have many fond memories of that old house."

After leaving the airport, Mr. Hopkins took Mary directly to her grandmother's house. Within a couple of days, all the arrangements had been made for Mary to take possession of her grandmother's personal property, including the house and car. Now came the task of sorting out what to keep and what to discard.

No one knew Mary had returned, except Mr. Hopkins. It had been Mary's decision not to tell anyone until after she had a chance to settle in and get a little organized.

MIKE FLANDERS WAS THE FIRST to find out that Mary had returned. He learned that Mary's grandmother had died from the local newspaper, and that she had lived on Stanley Street. It was not difficult for him to figure out that

Mary would come back to the house where she spent a lot of time as a young girl. He felt it would be only natural that she would stay there.

For weeks after the notice in the newspaper he kept a close watch on the house, waiting for Mary to return. Mike had always loved her. It did not matter to him that she did not even like him. It did not matter that she had reported his unwanted advances to the high school principal. He was sure she loved him, she just didn't realize it.

In his twisted mind, he knew he could win her over now that she had returned. He had convinced himself that he could make her love him if he planned his pursuit of her with care. He had waited years for this moment and knew just how to carry out his quest of Mary. This was not the first time he had pursued a woman, but he was convinced that he would succeed this time.

Mike's plan was simple, at least to him. Every day he would watch the house to see if anyone came to visit Mary. When the time was right, he would begin by scaring her just a little while she was alone. Then, when he felt she was scared enough, he would arrive on the scene to protect her much like a knight in shining armor. That would make her love him, he was sure of it.

He could remember how Mary liked being protected. John Blake, her high school sweetheart, was always there to make sure he never got to talk to her alone. But things would be different this time, Mike thought. John wasn't here to watch over her and get in his way. He knew that her brother was in the military and stationed somewhere out of the country. He also knew that Mary's parents had died in a car crash when she was in college. No one would be here to get in his way this time.

Though Mike's plan was filled with flaws, he was unable to see them. It was a simple plan and that was all that mattered to him. Complicated, complex plans were far beyond Mike's ability to reason or understand.

MIKE BEGAN HIS PLAN the very night that Mary returned. He discovered that there was a light on in the house. She had finally arrived and it was time to put his plan into action. He began by driving to her neighborhood and parking his car across the street. He would sit for hours just watching the house, waiting to see if anyone came by to visit her. He spent almost every evening just sitting and watching.

It seemed to Mike that Mary spent a great deal of time alone. She went out very little during the first week, and he had not seen anyone come to visit her. His plan was working perfectly. He decided it was time to find out what she was doing. The suspense was almost more than he could stand.

Late on Friday night of the second week, Mike parked his car around the corner from Mary's house. As he got out of the car, he looked around to make sure he had not been seen. When he felt it was safe, he snuck into the shadows of a nearby house.

Careful not to make any noise, he moved among the shadows from one house to the next until he was at the back of Mary's house. He worked his way along the side of the house. The first window he came to was open a few inches, but the drapes were drawn tight. He could not see in.

He moved on to the next window. That window was open and the drapes were pulled back. He could see Mary sitting at a desk. She had her back to him. Mike could not tell what she was doing at the desk. As he glanced around the room, he realized that she was sorting through the personal belongings of her grandmother.

As he watched her, all he could think about was how little she seemed to have changed. She was older, but still looked very much as she had in high school.

Mike was so absorbed in watching her that he didn't notice that he was being watched. The suddenness of a loud, deep male voice broke Mike's concentration.

"Hey, you! What the hell do you think you're doing?"

The rather gruff voice startled Mike. He looked toward the street and saw a large, older man standing on the sidewalk looking at him.

"Get the hell out of here! Damn Peeping Tom!" the man yelled.

Mike panicked and broke into a run. He ran around to the back of the house and into the next yard, jumping a small garden fence as he ran. As he ran through a yard, he was suddenly hit across the face with something very hard. Whatever it was that hit him, it knocked him off his feet and flat on his back. He hit the ground hard, knocking the wind out of him. He was stunned for a few seconds, and it took him a minute to catch his breath. He sat up and looked around. As it slowly registered in his mind, he realized that he must have run into a low hanging branch of a tree. He swore under his breath as he gathered himself up and began running toward his car. He didn't run quite as fast now for fear of running into another tree in the dark.

MARY HAD HEARD the man's voice, but didn't think anything of it until she heard a commotion outside her window. By the time she got to the window, Mike was gone. She raised the window up and looked out. Mr. McKenna, her neighbor, was standing on the sidewalk looking between the houses.

"What's going on, Mr. McKenna?"

"Oh, hi, Mary. It seems we have a Peeping Tom in the neighborhood."

"Did you see who it was?"

"No. I didn't get a good look at him. It's too dark. He sure took off in a hurry when I yelled at him, though," he said with a slight chuckle in his voice.

"You might want to keep your windows locked and your drapes closed at night," he suggested.

"I'll do that, and thank you for running him off."

Mr. McKenna just smiled, waved and then went on his way. Mary closed and locked the window, then closed the drapes. She felt uneasy knowing that someone had been watching her. It sent a cold chill down her spine. She couldn't understand why anyone would be interested in her and what she was doing. She tried to put the uneasy feeling aside, but it was difficult for her.

Mary returned to sorting through the items that had been left to her. Every now and then, she would turn her head and glance toward the window. Having had someone watching her made her jittery, and she didn't like the cold, chilling feeling it gave her.

WHEN MIKE REACHED HIS CAR, he quickly started it and sped off. He knew he had to get out of the neighborhood before someone saw him, or before he was reported to the police. If he got caught, his plans would be ruined.

It took him a few minutes to catch his breath. His nose and the side of his face were beginning to sting. He reached up and touched his nose then looked at his fingers. He could see blood on them.

"Damn," he said under his breath.

The tree branch had scratched his face. He needed to get to his apartment and clean up. Mike was also starting to get one of his stress headaches.

When he arrived at his apartment, he cleaned the scratches on his face and took some of the medication he had for his headache. He laid down on his bed in order to give it a chance to work and soon fell asleep.

BY TUESDAY OF THE THIRD WEEK, Mary started cleaning out the basement. In one of the storage rooms, she found several stacks of old clay flower pots. Most of them were of no value. She sorted the pots and stacked them outside the storage room. The good pots she would give to

Mrs. McKenna for her flowers, while the rest she would throw away. When she had finished sorting them, she picked up a handful of damaged pots and took them out to the trash container in the alley.

As she dumped the old cracked and broken pots in the trash, she noticed a car parked near the end of the alley. It was an old green station wagon. She hardly noticed it at first, but as she returned to the house it registered in her mind that she had seen that car in the neighborhood before. What struck her as strange was that it didn't seem to belong there. The car was old, its paint faded and it was rusty. This was one of the older neighborhood in town, but most of the cars were newer and in much better condition, and seemed to be parked in about the same place everyday.

Mary tried to put the car out of her mind and returned to the task at hand. When she returned with another armful of pots, she noticed the car was still there. She could see someone sitting in the car. She tried to pay little attention to the car, but with each trip to the trash container she became more apprehensive. Mary had no real reason to believe that whoever was in the car was watching her, but she couldn't help feeling that she was being watched.

Mary looked to see if anyone was around. She hoped Mr. McKenna would be working in his garden and would be where she could call to him. She wanted someone else to see the car. Maybe it was all in her imagination, she thought. Maybe she was just seeing things that were not really there. But the car was there and it was real, and the cold chill down her spine was just as real.

Mary quickly returned to the house. As soon as she was inside, she slammed and locked the door, then leaned back against it and took a deep breath. Why was the car so frightening to her? It was not unusual to see an old car like that around there. What was she so nervous about? She could not understand her feelings or the thoughts that ran wildly through her head. She had to mentally shake herself and pull herself together. Straightening her shoulders, she took a deep breath, then silently told herself that she was not going to let some old car upset her.

She looked down the stairs to the basement at the pile of old clay pots. Mary went down the stairs and collected another armful of pots. She made another trip to the trash container. After dumping the pots, she looked down the alley. The car was still there and there was someone sitting behind the wheel.

Determined not to let it get to her, she slammed the lid closed on the trash container and started walking toward the car. No matter how nervous or frightened she felt, she had to find out who was watching her and why.

As she moved closer, a cloud of blue-gray smoke came out from behind car as it was started. She still could not see who the driver was, but she was sure it was a man.

Suddenly, the car began to back down the alley away from her. It backed around the corner, then sped off east on Forest Street leaving a cloud of smoke behind. Mary nervously watched as the car disappeared. At least now she was sure she was being watched. Why else would he leave in such a hurry?

Mary wrapped her arms around herself. The day was warm, but she was feeling chilled inside. Why would someone be spying on her? What could she be doing that would be of interest to anyone else? Who was this man anyway? Of course, she had no answers to her questions. All she knew was it was making her nervous and very jumpy.

Mary found herself unable to concentrate, but she had convinced herself that she had to get things taken care of soon. There was really no reason for her to hurry, but keeping busy seemed to help keep her mind off what frightened her. Every time she went outside she would look up and down the alley, but she didn't see the car again. As the day went by, she began to feel as if she were making a big deal out of nothing. She had convinced herself that she had let her imagination get the best of her.

By dinnertime, Mary was feeling tired and dirty. After a late dinner, she went into the bathroom and took a leisurely shower. The warm water flowed over her body relaxing her tight muscles and relieving some of her tension. It also relieved the nervousness that had consumed her for a good part of the day. After showering, she wrapped her head with a towel and put on a soft robe. She returned to her bedroom and sat down in front of the dresser.

THAT EVENING, MIKE returned to Mary's neighborhood and parked his car a couple of blocks away. He carefully made his way to the back of her house again, being especially careful not to run into any tree branches. Working his way along side the house, he discovered that Mary's bedroom window was open a couple of inches but the drapes were closed. He could hear someone moving around in the room. He slowly slipped his hands inside the window and carefully separated the drapes just enough so he could see inside. Through the narrow opening in the drapes he could see Mary sitting in front of the mirror combing her hair.

Mary stood up and took off her robe, laying it across a chair. Mike took in a deep breath at the sight of her. The smoothness of her back, the curves of her hips and the shapeliness of her legs excited him. He watched her every move as she picked up her pink satin nightgown from the bed, slipped it over her head and let it cascade down her body.

He pulled back and ducked down below the window as Mary turned around. She did not notice the slight movement of the drapes as she walked toward the window. Pushing the drapes to one side, she closed the window, locked it, and then closed the drapes again.

Mike held his breath as he leaned against the house below the window. His heart was beating rapidly, but he remained quiet until the lights in her bedroom went out. He wanted her more then ever now that he had seen her.

Mike moved quickly and quietly away from the house. When he got to his car, he sat in it for a few minutes just thinking about Mary and how beautiful she still was after so many years. Several of the girls he had gone to high school with had lost their youthful figures within a few years after graduation, but not Mary. She was as pretty as ever.

With a clear vision of Mary on his mind, he drove to the gas station where he worked part-time. He put money in the phone and dialed a number. He listened as the phone began to ring.

MARY HAD NOT YET FALLEN asleep when the phone began to ring. She wondered who could be calling her at this hour. As far as she knew, Mr. Hopkins and the McKennas were the only ones who knew she was back. She turned on the bedside lamp and picked up the phone.

"Hello," she said, but there was no answer.

"Hello," she said a little louder, but still no answer.

She could hear what sounded like someone breathing. It made her nervous. She mustered up a little courage.

"Who is this?" she demanded.

"You will know soon enough," a whispery voice said. "I really like your pink nightgown, but I like you much better without it."

Mary was so startled and terrified that she dropped the phone as if it were too hot to hold. She looked at the window. Someone had been watching her get ready for bed. She suddenly realized that she should not have dismissed her earlier feelings so quickly. She did her best to gather up what courage she could and picked up the phone.

"Who are you? What do you want?" she demanded. She was unable to hide the fear from her voice.

"You will find out soon enough. I'm watching you," the voice whispered.

"Leave me alone! You're sick!" she yelled into the receiver, then slammed it down.

Mike hung up the phone and smiled to himself. Things were going as planned. She was scared, just like he wanted her to be. He returned to his car and drove to his apartment, very much satisfied with himself.

MARY FELT A COLD CHILL slide down her spine again. She pulled the covers up around her neck as she looked around the room. What was going on? Who was doing this to her? Whoever it was, he was a very sick person. The thought that this degenerate might be a dangerous psychopath didn't escape her mind, either. In fact, it was the thought of it that frightened her even more.

She got out of bed and quickly put on her robe. She hurried from room to room making sure that every door and every window was closed and locked. When she returned to the bedroom, she got into bed keeping her robe on. She pulled it tightly around her as if it would protect her. She was so frightened that every sound she heard made her jump. It was hours before she finally fell asleep, and only then because of pure exhaustion.

OVER THE NEXT FEW DAYS, she jumped at every little noise. The sound of the paper landing on the front porch, a tree branch rubbing against the house in the wind, an unexpected noise from a car, even a door shutting made her jump. She found it impossible to concentrate on anything.

During that time, Mary had seen the old car in the neighborhood several more times, always in a different place. No matter how hard she tried to see the driver, it was always too far away. Once, she almost got close enough to see the driver, but he ducked down and sped away before she could get a good look at him.

LATE SATURDAY NIGHT of the fourth week, Mike drove slowly past Mary's house. After circling the block several times, he was convinced she had gone to bed. He parked his car down the street, then walked to Mary's house. He ducked behind some bushes. When he was certain it was safe, he moved in the shadows toward her front door.

Hiding behind an evergreen, he pulled a note from his pocket. He had made the note by pasting letters from the local newspaper onto a piece of paper. He took a tack from his pocket and carefully tacked the note to Mary's front door.

Mike looked around to see if anyone was watching, then moved away from the house and returned to his car. He felt very good as he started back to his apartment in Depot Town. He also felt a twinge of disappointment that he would not be there to see the expression on Mary's face or her reaction when she opened the door and found the note.

"Oh, well," he said to himself, "it will work, and that's all that really matters."

CHAPTER TWO

SUNDAY MORNING ARRIVED with a gentle breeze and the sun shining brightly. Soft billowy clouds floated across the sky. It promised to be a beautiful day with only a slight chance of a late afternoon shower.

Mary woke still feeling tired. She had not slept well. After making herself a cup of coffee, she went to the front door to retrieve the Sunday paper from the porch. When she turned to go back into the house, she saw the note tacked to the door. She removed the note and read it. A chill rushed through her entire body causing her to almost panic.

Pulling her robe tightly around her, she quickly looked around, but saw no one. Mary knew that she was being watched every minute, but by whom and from where? She stepped back inside, then quickly shut the door, locked it and leaned back against the door as if to hold it shut. She did not understand what was happening, but whatever it was it was slowly driving her crazy. She knew that she could not take much more of this. She had to do something about it, but what?

Mary tried to pull her thoughts together as her body trembled in fear. She returned to the kitchen and tried to pick up her coffee cup, but she was shaking so badly that she spilled part of it. She sat down at the table and instantly broke into tears.

It took several minutes before calm slowly began to return. She remembered that going to church had always helped her in a time of need. There was no doubt that this was a time of need for her. Spending time in the quiet of a church might be just what she needed to help her think, to calm her nerves and help her to think logically.

She returned to her bedroom and picked out what she would wear, but not before she checked each window to make sure it was not only closed, but locked. Then she secured the drapes so no one could see in.

As soon as she was ready, she went outside. Mary took a minute to look around before she stepped off the porch and quickly got into her car, locking the doors immediately. She backed out of the drive and started for church. A glance at the gas gauge told her that she needed to stop for fuel. Mary stopped at the Amoco Station at the corner of Cross and Prospect Streets. She was looking in her purse when a man walked up to the car.

"Hi, Mary."

Mary jumped, spilling the contents of her purse. She turned and looked at the face looking in her car window. They were only inches apart. The first thing she saw were the ugly scabs on the side of his face and across the bridge of his nose. She instantly felt that same cold chill rush through her.

"It's me, Mike Flanders," he said with a grin.

Mary stared at him for several seconds before she recognized him. She was frozen with fear and unable to move. Panic suddenly gripped at her heart and squeezed it, taking her breath away. She felt a sudden and urgent need to flee, to get away from him.

In a desperate attempt to get away, she slammed the car into gear and stepped hard on the gas pedal. The car jumped forward and sped out onto Cross Street.

Mike had to jump back away from the car in order to keep her from running over his feet as she peeled out. He watched as Mary's car sped on down the street. He smiled as he thought of how successfully his plan was working so far.

Mary had gone several blocks before she was able to gather enough of her senses to realize she was speeding. She slowed the car down and then pulled over to the curb and stopped. Resting her forehead on the steering wheel, she tried to catch her breath. Instead, tears began rolling down her cheeks as she cried uncontrollably. She was feeling so very helpless, so very much alone and so afraid.

After she regained some of her composure and felt she could drive again, Mary turned the car around and drove straight home. She pulled into the driveway and shut off the engine. Afraid that her legs wouldn't carry her into the house, she sat in the car for a few minutes with her head against the steering wheel.

"I can't continue to live like this," she cried out loud.

Everything that moved or made a sound frightened her. She was sure that it would not be long before she would end up in a mental hospital if she didn't get some help soon.

MARY FINALLY LIFTED her head from the steering wheel and looked at her purse. It was still lying on the floor of the car. Taking a deep breath, she bent down and began picking up everything that had fallen out. She didn't hear the car stop in front of the house, or see the woman get out and walk toward her.

"Hi, Kido."

The blonde's voice showed her excitement in seeing Mary again. But Mary just about jumped out of her skin for the second time in less than an hour. Once again she dropped her purse. Mary turned to see who it was. Seeing her old friend, Kay Sinclair, she leaned back in the seat and tipped her head back against the headrest. She closed her eyes while she took a minute to catch her breath and get her heart beating regularly again.

"What's the matter with you? My God, you're jumpy."

"God, Kay, you scared the hell out of me!"

"I'm sorry, but it's more than that. I've never known you to be jumpy."

"You're right," Mary conceded quietly. "I need to talk to someone. Come inside, please?"

"Sure."

Kay went around to the other side of the car and helped Mary pick up what had spilled from her purse. Mary stuffed everything back in her purse, then Kay walked with Mary to the house.

"You look like you haven't been getting enough sleep," Kay said, her concern for Mary showing on her face.

"You're right about that, but it's not just the lack of sleep," Mary admitted.

Mary tried to put things into perspective before telling Kay too much, but without much luck. She didn't want it to sound worse than it was, but than it could not get much worse, she reasoned.

Kay watched Mary, and was curious to know what she was muttering about. Following her into the house, Kay noticed that Mary immediately locked the door as soon as they were inside.

"Ok, Mary, what's wrong? I've known you a long time, and I've never known you to lock the door during the day, especially when you are at home. Is this something you learned in South America?"

"No," she sighed. "Kay, someone has been watching me."

"Who's been watching you?"

"I don't know," she said with a hint of frustration in her voice.

"How do you know you're being watched?"

"I had a note left on my door this morning telling me that I am being watched. I've gotten telephone calls telling me that I'm being watched. There's an old green station wagon in the neighborhood at all hours of the day, and in different places all the time. Mr. McKenna caught a Peeping Tom at my window one night and ran him off. It's about to drive me crazy."

Mary's frustration and fear showed clearly in her voice as well as on her face.

"The note, what did it say?" Kay's interest was rising fast.

"It said I was being watched. That's all."

"Do you have any idea who it might be?"

"No. Hardly anyone knows I'm back. Do you think I would be just sitting here if I knew who was doing this to me?" Mary asked, her voice showing her fear and her frustration.

"I'm sorry, I didn't mean to give you the third degree. Have you called the police?"

"No. What can they do? Whoever it is hasn't really threatened me. He hasn't broken into my house or my car. He's just been watching me. I'm scared, Kay."

Mary's eyes pleaded for help.

"Come and stay with us for a few days. Tom will be glad to see you."

Mary thought about it for a minute. If she stayed with Kay and her husband, she wouldn't be alone and she might get some rest. It would be a relief to get away, if only for a few days.

"Okay," she relented after thinking about it for a minute. "I can't seem to get anything done here anyway."

Kay followed Mary into the bedroom and helped Mary pack a few things, then took them to the car. Mary made sure all the doors and windows of the house where locked before leaving.

Mary got in her car and followed Kay onto Prospect. As she drove through the intersection of Cross and Prospect streets, she caught sight of something out of the corner of her eye. That almost too familiar cold chill ran through her when she noticed a rusty old beat up green station wagon parked at the gas station. A sharp pang of fear made her hands tighten on the steering wheel and her heart beat faster. She could feel sweat break out on her forehead.

Mary's mind filled with questions. What was happening to her? What if that was the same green car? Maybe it belonged to someone who lived in the neighborhood. It would make sense if it was being serviced at a neighborhood service station, but she quickly realized that the Amoco station was no longer a service station. It was now a convenience store.

In her current state of mind, Mary couldn't be sure of anything. The more she thought about it, the more confusing the whole thing was becoming to her.

Suddenly, Mary felt very tired. It was probably a good idea for her to spend a few days with Kay and Tom, she decided. She certainly would feel much more secure with friends close by, and a little rest wouldn't hurt, either. She also decided that it might be better to say as little as possible about what had been happening until she could sort it out in her own mind and try to make some sense of it herself.

KAY TURNED INTO THE driveway of a very nice ranch style home on Browning Street. The two-car garage door was open and in the garage was a green car up on blocks. Mary looked at the car as she parked in front of the house. God, there must be a million green cars around, she thought.

Kay walked over to Mary's car. The concerned look on Kay's face let Mary know that Kay was worried about her. Mary smiled as she got out of her car. Her smile was a feeble attempt to hide her fears.

"It's funny, but as we drove over here I noticed a number of green cars. Even my best friend has a green car."

"That's Tom's old car. He's been working on it for years. I don't know if he'll ever get it finished," Kay replied with a grin.

"Kay, let's not say anything to Tom just yet, please. I'm very tired, and I'm not ready to talk about it. If I can get some rest, then maybe we can talk. Okay?"

"Okay, but Tom will guess there's something wrong when he sees you."

"Is it that obvious?"

"Yes. You have dark circles under your eyes, you look tired, and you're jumpy as hell. It's that obvious."

"Okay, okay, I get the message. But if I don't get some rest before we talk, I'll probably just break down and cry," Mary said in frustration.

"All right, I'll tell him you've been working too hard. He'll understand. Come on. You can use the spare bedroom."

Kay picked up Mary's clothes bag and led the way. Just as Mary entered the house, Kay turned and put her finger over her lips.

"Tom's where he often is on Sunday, asleep in his chair in front of the TV," Kay whispered.

Kay led Mary down the hall to the bedroom.

"You can use this room for as long as you want."

"Thanks, Kay. I really appreciate this."

"That's okay. What are friends for? You want something to eat?"

"No. I just want to rest.

"Okay. You get some rest. When you get up, we'll have dinner, then we can talk," Kay said as she laid Mary's clothes bag on the chest at the foot of the bed.

"Okay," Mary replied.

Kay left the room, leaving Mary alone. Mary set her overnight case on the chest beside her clothes bag. After stripping to her underwear, she pulled the covers back and crawled under them. For the first time in weeks, she felt as though she might be able to get some sleep. She felt safe and secure here, a feeling she missed these past few weeks.

Now that she was feeling a little more secure, Mary's thoughts slowly turned to another time and to the one person she had always been able to lean on when she needed someone.

She closed her eyes as she remembered those days when John Blake had meant everything in the world to her. He had always made her feel safe and protected, yet he never smothered her. The thought of "where is John now" passed through her mind.

In a very short time Mary was asleep, off in a dream world of her own. She dreamt of a day years ago that she had spent with John. A day that had been peaceful and pleasant for her.

JOHN TOOK THE CANOE off the top of his car and carried it to the riverbank. Mary had been watching him, and she was sure that he knew it. She was also sure he didn't mind.

He smiled at her as he walked toward her.

"You ready?"

"Yes," she replied.

He held the canoe as she stepped in and moved to the bow. As soon as she was seated, he pushed off as he stepped in and sat down.

Mary picked up her paddle and began reaching way out in front of her to take long hard strokes. After a few strokes, she looked over her shoulder and smiled at John. She knew he had been canoeing for years, but today was her first time.

"Am I holding this right?" she asked as she held up the paddle.

"You're holding it just fine, but you might not want to take such long strokes. Do it more like this," he said as he demonstrated a shorter, smoother stroke.

She turned back around and tried to paddle like he had shown her. She found it much easier, and they seemed to move along just as well.

"How's that? Is it easier?"

"Yes. Canoeing is not that hard."

For the next hour or so, they paddled leisurely down the Huron River. The sun was bright, but most of the time they were in the shade of the large oak, maple and elm trees that lined the shore of the river. In the shade, it was cool and refreshing. Mary enjoyed the peace and quiet on the river. There was an occasional bird that would fly up, or a small splash from a fish breaking the surface of the water, or a turtle diving off a log.

Mary had been paddling along at a steady pace, and was beginning to feel it in her shoulders and back. She laid the paddle across the canoe in front of her and tried to loosen up her shoulder as she looked around.

"Tired?" John asked.

Mary could hear the concern for her in John's voice. She turned and looked back at him.

"I'm not used to this," she said not wanting him to think of her as a wimp.

"Take it easy. We're in no hurry. We have all day."

"I want to do my share."

"If you're not used to canoeing, it's very easy to get blisters and sore muscles. Take your time and paddle when you want."

Mary knew there was no hurry. Besides, it was too nice a day to hurry. The large patches of water lilies close to the shore of the river were full of their white flowers, the cattails were standing tall along the bank, and the leaves of the trees were swaying gently in the breeze.

"Are you getting hungry?" John asked.

"I could eat anytime now."

"Up ahead there's a big oak tree on the right. We could have our lunch there."

"Is that it?" she asked at the sight of a lone giant oak.

"That's it."

Mary took a few strokes with the paddle as John steered the canoe toward the tree. The tree's branches spread out over the river like an umbrella. Underneath the tree was a short thick mat of grass and a strip of sand forming a narrow beach.

The bow of the canoe slid up on the sandy beach. Mary got out and held the rope while John stepped out of the canoe. He took the rope and pulled the canoe far enough up onto the beach so that it would not float away.

Mary found it hard to believe that there was such a place as this so close to town. It was like finding a small piece of paradise. The grass was soft and cool under her bare feet. When she turned to look at John, she found him watching her. She smiled and moved toward him. She reached out and put her hands on his shoulders while he slipped his hands around her narrow waist and drew her to him.

"This is a beautiful place," she said as she looked up at him.

"I thought you would like it. Would you like to go swimming before lunch?"

"Yes," she replied then rose up on her tiptoes and kissed him lightly on the lips.

After such a tender kiss, John was obviously reluctant to let go of her. After letting go of her, he retrieved a blanket from the canoe and spread it out under the tree.

They had come prepared to go swimming. Mary took off her blouse and shorts revealing a black one-piece swimming suit. She watched John take off his shirt and shorts. She thought John looked very nice in his blue swimming trunks. In fact, it even crossed her mind that he looked a little sexy.

It was clear to her that John thought she looked very nice in her swimming suit, too. It embarrassed her just a little to have him look at her like he was. It was not so much from the fact that he was looking at her, but because she liked to have him look at her.

John took her by the hand and led her into the river. The water was cool, but it felt good. They swam out into the river. When Mary stopped and stood up, John swam to her and wrapped his arms around her. She put her arms around his neck and tilted her head back. He leaned down and kissed her.

Mary could feel the warmth of his body pressed against her. It raised an awareness of John that she had only had a hint of a time or two before. She knew she loved him, but she felt a special kind of comfort in his arms, as if this was where she belonged. Her love for John was very special and went deep into the recesses of her heart.

After a long kiss, they waded out of the river. Hand in hand they walked over to where John had laid out the blanket. Sitting on the blanket, they ate their lunch. She watched John as if she had come to realize that he was the one person for her.

John gathered up the leftovers and packed them back in the picnic basket. Mary laid down on the blanket and closed her eyes. John laid down beside her, his hands behind his head. She turned and looked at him, then rolled up against him. He wrapped his arm around her and held her close.

Mary rested her head on his shoulder. She felt very safe and secure in his arms. She closed her eyes and found a quiet peaceful feeling filled her senses.

MARY SLOWLY OPENED her eyes. It had been a long time since she felt as rested and relaxed as she did at that moment. She knew she had been dreaming, but her dream had helped her get the rest she needed. She felt a wave of disappointment wash over her now that her dream was over.

The room was dark and she had no idea what time it was, but she had slept well past dinner. She turned the lamp on and looked at her watch. It was after nine o'clock. She got up and dressed again. As she walked out into the hall, she could hear voices coming from the family room.

"Hi," she said as she entered the family room.

"Hi, sleepyhead. Did you get a good rest?" Tom asked.

"Oh, yes. I feel much better, but I'm kind of hungry."

"Well, let's get you something to eat," Kay said as she led the way to the kitchen.

"Kay tells me that you're being watched by someone in a green car," Tom said as he followed Mary to the kitchen.

"I don't think it's as bad as I made it sound. My neighbor did see a Peeping Tom outside my window and ran him off, and someone put a note on my door telling me I was being watched."

Mary sat down at the counter while Kay got out something for her to eat.

"As for the green car, I don't know. I must have seen a dozen green cars just between your place and mine," Mary said trying to keep from making it sound worse than it was. "I think it was mostly my imagination."

"I think we should call the police, Tom Suggested. "I have a friend on the force that would be glad to check it out for you."

"No, I don't want you to call him. I just need some time to rest and get away from the house for a little while. I think the combination of being tired, and the depressing nature of what I have had to do, has made me a little out of sorts," Mary said in an effort to explain.

"Okay. You stay here for a few days, and stay away from the house until you've had a chance to get rested up. Maybe I can help you later in the week," Kay suggested.

"I think we should take Mary to the Class Reunion dance next Saturday. It will be a good diversion for her, and she will get to see a few old school friends she hasn't seen for years," Tom suggested.

"Oh, I don't know. I don't know if I'll feel up to it," Mary protested.

"I think it will do you good. Besides, you even admitted you've been working too hard," Kay said.

"Okay. I promise I'll think about it." Mary said reluctantly.

"Okay, that's good enough for now."

Mary knew that when the time came to go to the Class Reunion dance, she would most likely go. She didn't feel like it was the thing she really wanted to do, but maybe by the weekend she might feel differently. Deep down she knew that she would go.

After a couple of days of rest, Mary was feeling much better. There were no phone calls in the middle of the night, no notes left on the door, and no old green cars around, except for Tom's.

THE DAY OF THE CLASS REUNION turned out to be a very nice day. Mary decided to drive by the house to make sure all was well before getting ready to go. As she pulled into the drive, she noticed another note tacked on the door. The cold chill that ran down her spine was way too familiar.

Seeing the note, she didn't even get out of the car. She simply started the car up again and drove straight back to Kay and Tom's house. She went directly to her room without a word to anyone. She sat on the edge of the bed, put her face in her hands and cried.

After her nerves had a chance to calm down and she was able to think rationally again, she got dressed for the dance. Mary had no desire to go, but she was determined not to spoil the evening for Kay and Tom. They had been so nice to her that she couldn't do that to them. She was not sure she could keep them from knowing something was wrong, but she wouldn't say anything until after the dance. Once the dance was over, she would ask Tom to call his policeman friend. She couldn't take much more. She had to do something to put a stop it.

CHAPTER THREE

IT WAS A WARM SUMMER afternoon when John Blake turned his bright red convertible off Interstate 94 on to a two-lane country road. The sky was blue with a few billowy clouds floating across it. It seemed almost a sin to drive along such a beautiful country road with the top up. John found a wide place in the road, pulled over and stopped. He put the top down, then drove on with the wind in his hair and the sun on his face.

John felt good being back in Michigan, the place where he had grown up. His thoughts turned to the many times that Bill Jordan and he had gone camping in the woods and along several of the rivers in the area. They had had a lot of fun sitting around campfires and canoeing along the rivers. Isn't it strange the things one thinks of at times like these, he thought to himself?

John smiled to himself as he remembered a time when Bill almost let the canoe get away and float down the river without them. He also remembered a time when they canoed around a bend in the river and found Penny Shaffer and a couple of her girl friends swimming nude in the river. He smiled at the thought of Penny's friends screaming as they ran for cover while Penny stayed in the water. He could almost hear her sexy voice when she invited Bill to come and swim with her. Bill reluctantly declined.

JOHN WAS NOW ALONE. His children were on their own and his wife of many years had passed away. Now that he had the time and the money from years of hard work, he had no one to share it with. Life wasn't always fair, John thought, but than he wasn't one to let it get him down for very long.

John, at the age of forty-five, was still young enough to enjoy life. He had invested his money wisely and decided to retire, at least for a while. He would do some of the things he had always wanted to do but never seemed to have the time. His first stop would be to visit his old high school buddy and his wife. When he called to tell them he was coming back to Michigan for a visit, John was invited to stay with Bill and his wife, Julie.

John turned off the road into the driveway leading to Bill and Julie Jordan's house and stopped in front of the garage. As he was getting out of the car, Julie came to the door and stepped out onto the deck.

"Hi, John," Julie called out as she waved to him.

"Hi, Julie. Where's that bum you married?"

"He's coming. He's in the basement working on my toaster. I don't think he will be able to fix it this time. I told him we should just get a new one, but he thinks he can make it work."

"Well, I can make it work," Bill said as he came up behind her.

"Hi, John. How was the trip?"

"Come inside before you get started on that," Julie interrupted.

They went inside the house and spent time talking about John's trip and the upcoming Class Reunion. John was reluctant to go. He had little interest in big gatherings.

"Come on, John, why not go with us? Give me one good reason why you don't want to go?" Bill asked.

"Hell, Bill, I'd feel like a fifth wheel. I hardly know anyone round here anymore. I've been gone from here for so many years."

John was feeling a little frustrated, but he didn't want to argue with Bill.

"You and Julie go and have a good time. Don't worry about me. I'll stay here and keep the dog company."

"John Blake, the dog doesn't need company. You'll come with us to the dance, or we'll all stay home," Julie promised.

"Besides, how are you going to find some of the people you went to school with if you don't go? You won't find a better place to get information on old school friends than at a high school class reunion. You never know, some of them might even be there," Bill added.

"Okay, okay, I give up," John exclaimed holding his hands up in surrender. "I'll go, but you have to promise me that you won't let me ruin your evening because I don't have a date. Is it a deal?"

"It's a deal," Julie agreed.

They spent the better part of the afternoon talking about everything from what they had done over the past couple of years, to politics, to sports. The afternoon went by fast for all of them. It was soon time to get ready for the Class Reunion dance.

John went to the bathroom to shower and shave then went to the guest bedroom to get dressed. While he was dressing, his thoughts turned to a girl he hadn't thought about for a long time, Mary Weston. He still remembered her clearly. She had meant a great deal to him.

Without any difficulty he could picture her in his mind as if she were standing in front of him at this very minute. During their high school years, she had worn her brown hair kind of short. Her eyes were a deep dark brown and seemed to sparkle all the time. She was five foot, four inches tall and had a very nice figure.

Although he could remember a good deal about her, he couldn't remember their last date, or what had caused them to break up. John couldn't remember anything traumatic, such as a big fight over who knows what. As he could best remember, it seemed that they had simply drifted apart the summer between their Junior and Senior years of high school. He could remember that she had been very special to him, and he had loved her very much.

John made no effort to control his thoughts. He simply let his mind wander. He could remember many of the things they had done, the places that they had gone, and the friends they shared. While he was combing his hair, one very special time came to mind as clearly as if it had happened yesterday. It was a time that reminded him of how much she had meant to him.

JOHN AND MARY HELD HANDS as they walked along the sidewalk on Stanley Street and turned up the walk to her grandmother's house. At the front door, John handed Mary her books and kissed her lightly. Stepping back, he smiled at her.

"I guess I'll see you at school in the morning."

"My grandmother won't be home for at least an hour, would you like to come in?" Mary's voice was soft as she spoke to him. Her sparkling brown eyes invited him to stay.

"Sure, but I don't want your folks to have any reason to keep us from going to the dance after the game Friday night."

"Just for a little while," she said with a smile.

John smiled and followed her into the house. She took his hand and led him to the basement family room. He picked out some records and put them on the phonograph. As soon as the first song began to play, John turned to Mary.

"Would you like to dance?"

She smiled at him, then stepped in front of him. She put her arms around his neck as he pulled her up against him, and they began to move with the music. Her hair smelled fresh and felt soft. It felt good to hold her in his arms. As she looked up at him, he leaned down and kissed her lightly on the lips.

When the music stopped, John led her to the sofa and sat down. Mary sat on his lap, placed an arm around his neck and a hand on his cheek as she looked into his eyes.

John wrapped an arm around her narrow waist and laid his other arm across her lap, resting his hand on her hip. He tipped his head up as she leaned down toward him, gently sliding her hand to the back of his neck. Once again their lips met in a warm, tender kiss.

Gradually their kisses grew deeper and stronger, with their lips pressing harder and harder against each other. John slowly moved his arm from her back to her side, with his fingers gradually moving along the side of her breast. A soft moan came from deep inside her as she became aware of his touch.

Mary pulled away and looked down at him. She gently ran the palm of her hand over his cheek and whispered, "I love you."

"I love you, too," he whispered.

Looking into John's eyes, she took hold of his hand. She placed his hand over her breast and held it there. They looked into each other's eyes for what seemed like forever. Their hearts began to beat faster and their breathing grew deeper. She took her hand off his and slid it behind his neck, then leaned down and kissed him again. Their mouths opened and their tongues touched. She moaned softly as he moved his hand over her firm breast.

As they kissed, John slid his hand down her side and under her sweater. He guided his hand up her side to the satiny material of her bra. As he slid his hand over her breast again, she took in a deep breath. Her body tensed for a few seconds, then she pulled back. Looking up at her face, he could see that she liked the way he was touching her.

She opened her eyes and looked into his. Without saying a word, she took her arms from around his neck. She crossed her arms in front of her body and took hold of the bottom of her sweater. In one smooth move, she pulled her sweater up over her head. She dropped the sweater on the sofa next to him, then sat quietly with her arms at her sides.

Mary reached out and unbuttoned John's shirt. Placing her hands under his shirt, she pushed it off his shoulders and down his arms. When she had his shirt off, she cupped his face in her hands and gently tipped his face up. She held his face in her hands as they kissed again.

John kissed her lips, her chin and on down to her neck. Mary tipped her head back and put her hands behind his head. She guided his kisses down to the swell of her breasts.

John slowly slid his hand up off her breast to her shoulder. He took one of her shoulder straps of her bra in his fingers and slowly pushed it off her shoulder. As the strap slid down her arm, the soft material rolled off her breast. Her breath caught as the cool air swept over her naked breast.

He looked down at her breast and watched it rise and fall with each breath she took. He cupped her breast in his hand and gently felt it. John had never wanted any girl more than he wanted her at that moment.

Reluctantly, he took his hand from her breast and slowly pushed the strap of her bra back up over her shoulder. The soft material of her bra once again covered her firm young breast.

Mary looked at him with an expression he would never forget. He could see the hurt and disbelief in her eyes. She loved him so much that she was willing to give herself to him, and he had turned her away. Tears began to fill her eyes.

"I love you," he said in almost a whisper, "You are so beautiful. I want you. I want you more than I could ever tell you. But not now, not like this. I want you when we are both ready. I want you when both of us are ready to make a commitment to each other, not just for now, but forever.

"When we make love, it should be something very special. It should be when we can stay together, not for just a few minutes on a sofa in your grandmother's basement."

He tried to explain, desperately wanting her to understand what he wasn't sure he understood himself. He searched her eyes for some kind of clue to tell him that she understood. He wanted so much for her to believe in him, to trust in him, and for her to love him as much as he loved her. It hurt him deeply to see the tears in her eyes and the hurt look on her face.

Slowly the hurt look on Mary's face gave way to a soft smile. The love he had been able to see in her eyes had returned. Her eyes told him that she understood why he would not make love to her now. They told him that she knew how much he loved her, and that he cared very much about her.

"I love you," she said in soft whisper.

Mary wrapped her arms around him and kissed him with more tenderness and love than he had ever known. After a long kiss, she pulled back and looked at him. He reached up and gently wiped the tears from her cheek. Her face seemed to glow with her love for him. He slid his hand off her back, picked up her sweater and handed it to her.

"I think you better put this on before I change my mind."

Mary took the sweater and stood up. She moved to the other side of the coffee table, stopped and turned toward him as he stood up. She hesitated for a moment before putting her sweater on. John put his shirt on as he watched her pull her sweater down over her head.

John moved around the coffee table and stood in front of her. He reached out and put his hands on her narrow waist. As she put her hands on his shoulders, he drew her close.

"I better be going before your grandmother gets home."

"Meet me at my locker in the morning?"

"Yes. I'll miss you tonight," he said softly as he squeezed her against him.

"I'll miss you, too," she replied as she slid her arms around his neck.

He leaned down and kissed her soft lips and held her tightly. The kiss they shared was long and loving, expressing a deep love between them.

"HEY, JOHN, ARE YOU READY to go?" Bill called from downstairs.

"Be right down."

John took a quick check of how he looked in the mirror.

"Here I come, ready or not," he called back.

Bill and Julie were standing at the bottom of the stairs as he came down. Julie was wearing a white blouse with delicate lace around the neck, a plain green skirt and matching green shoes.

"Julie, you look great," John said.

Bill had on a pair of gray slacks, light blue dress shirt with a red tie and a dark blue blazer. Bill and John could have passed for twins. Except for the color of their ties, they were dressed alike.

"My men look very nice tonight," Julie said as she took each of them by an arm and led them toward the door.

On the drive to the Hoyt Meeting Center, John had trouble concentrating on their conversation. He kept thinking of Mary and wondered what had happened to her. He wondered what she had been doing since he last saw her some twenty or more years ago.

JOHN, BILL AND JULIE ARRIVED at the Hoyt Meeting Center about seven o'clock. The class reunion was scheduled to open for arrivals at seven-thirty with the music to begin at eight o'clock. Since Bill and Julie were on the sign-in committee, they had to check people in for the first hour.

"John, why don't you find us a table, and we'll join you as soon as our replacements arrive," Bill suggested.

"First, let's get you checked in," Julie said.

Julia wrote his name on a piece of paper and pinned it to a board so everyone could see who had come to the reunion.

"Do you think anyone will remember me?"

"I think you'll be surprised," Bill replied.

"There are only a few I would be interested in knowing what has happened to them," John remarked.

"Well, maybe some of them will show up tonight," Julie said with her usual optimism.

John nodded his head in agreement, then went into the meeting room. He picked out a table near the windows, then went out on the patio to look around. From there he could see the old Peninsular Paper Mill, or at least what was left of it, down by the river, and the light from the setting sun reflecting off the water.

This could be a very romantic place if the right person were here, he thought. The thought flashed through his mind that the right person could be Mary Weston.

Questions kept coming to mind. Questions he couldn't answer. What was it that kept him thinking about her? Was it the fact that he had returned to Michigan after so many years? Was it the fact that he was lonely for someone who knew him? Or was there some other reason he was unable to understand?

JOHN WENT BACK INSIDE and sat down. A few people had started coming in. The first few he didn't think he knew, but he really wasn't paying much attention.

"You're John Blake, aren't you?"

The voice was loud and clear. He thought he should recognize that voice, but couldn't place it. John certainly didn’t recognize the person.

"Yes," John said as he turned and looked up at the rather short, round, bald man standing next to him. John could not place him. The woman standing next to the man was almost as round, but she did look a little familiar.

"I'll bet you don't know who I am?"

The man seemed to be almost yelling, but John was sure it was just the way he talked. He knew he should recognize that silly grin, but still couldn't place it.

"I think you would win that bet," John said not feeling much like playing guessing games. "I should know you, but..."

John was not really interested in who this loud-mouthed little man might be. In fact, he was hoping the man would simply go away.

"I'm Chuck Martin. And this is my wife, the former Sharon Wentworth," he stated proudly.

John could hardly believe his eyes. This chubby little woman standing next to his table had once been one of the sexiest girls in high school. She had had a figure and face that made most of the boys drool. It was hard to believe that she had changed so much.

"Well, I'll be darned. I never would have guessed."

As John remembered it, they had not been friends in high school. They had not even run around in the same circle of friends. If John's memory served him right, Chuck was as much a loudmouth back then as he appeared to be now.

John heard someone call Chuck from across the room. Without a word, Chuck turned and waved, then simply walked away. Sharon smiled at John, turned, and followed her husband across the room.

John was glad to see them leave, but he couldn't keep from watching Sharon as they walked away. She followed her husband across the room as if she were required to walk two paces behind. During high school, she would not have followed anyone. John never would have guessed that Sharon "the boobs" Wentworth would have ended up with Chuck "the loudmouth" Martin. Strange things happen, he thought.

John turned and looked toward the entrance just in time to see a woman walk in who he was sure he should know. He watched her as she walked across the room. She was tall and slim, and so was the man with her. John knew that he should know the woman, but couldn't think of her name. He didn't think he knew the man, but in a way he looked familiar, too.

John got up from the table and started across the room. About halfway across, it came to him who the woman was. She had kept her slim figure and good looks very well through the years, but he still couldn't place the man with her. As he approached their table, she looked up. A big smile came over her face when she saw him.

"You're Charlotte Frasier aren't you?"

"Yes, but its Mrs. Frank Armstrong now."

"I'm John Blake. Would I be right if I said this is Frank Armstrong?" John reached out to shake hands.

"That's right. Please, sit down," Frank said as he stood up and shook John's hand.

"Well, just for a minute. I came with Bill and Julie Jordan. They will be joining me soon."

"We saw them at the sign-in desk."

"Tell me, what have you been up to for the last twenty years or so?"

"Frank and I got married right after college. We have two very lovely children. One is in college at the University of Michigan, and the other will graduate from high school next year. Frank is a vice president for Coler Electronics in Detroit."

"Sounds like things have gone well for you. What do you hear from the old gang? I haven't seen anyone from high school since I left for the service, except for Karen. I saw her about - - oh - - fifteen years ago. She had two kids and was divorced."

"I heard from her about a month ago. She is married to a nice man who is some years older," Charlotte said.

"Tom, - ah - Tom Lamb, was married and is now divorced. He's a college professor at Northern, I believe. You remember Mike, Mike, ah, Flanders, that's it, Mike Flanders. I know he didn't run around in the same crowd, but he still lives around here. I think he works at the Amoco station on the corner of Cross and Prospect. He's a maintenance man, or something."

"Oh, I remember Flanders," John replied. "I got into a fight with him just before the Senior Prom. If I hadn't had witnesses to say he started it, I might have been suspended."

"I think Karen would have killed you if you couldn't have taken her to the Prom. She was really upset with you over that. The last time I talked to Karen, she said that she might come to the dance tonight, but I haven't seen her yet. She'll be glad to see you again," Charlotte added.

Just then, Bill and Julie came across the room to the table. John was a little disappointed. He was about to ask Charlotte if she knew what had happened to Mary.

"Hi, Charlotte."

Bill was pleasant, but he seemed to be in a hurry.

"I hope you don't mind, but I need to talk to John for a minute."

Charlotte and Frank nodded as if they understood what it was all about. John gave a half-hearted wave, then left the room with Bill and Julie.

BILL TOOK JOHN'S ARM and led him off into a corner of the room. He drew him up close and looked around before he spoke.

"Do you know who's here?"

"What's going on?" John was confused by the urgency shown in Bill's actions.

"Do you know who's here?"

It had been so long since he had been in this part of the country that he couldn't think of who they could possibly be talking about. He simply shrugged his shoulders in reply.

"Mike Flanders is here. He saw your name on the board at the sign-in table and turned as pale as a ghost," Julie said.

There was a hint of worry in her statement. John didn't know Julie very well, but she didn't seem to be the type who would worry over nothing.

"So?" John didn't see why that bit of information should be so important that he needed to be told in secret.

"When Mike saw your name on the board, we got the impression that he was extremely upset to see you were here," Bill stated.

"My God, Bill, it's been over twenty years. Do you really think he still holds a grudge?"

John couldn't believe that they were making such a big deal of this.

"You didn't see the look in his eyes when he saw your name. We did," Julie said, the tone of her voice showing that she was serious.

The fact that it upset Julie was enough to make John think. He felt it might be wise to be careful around Mike. He was sure there was nothing to worry about, but a little caution certainly couldn't hurt.

"What are you going to do?" Julie asked.

"Unless he starts something, I don't plan to do anything. He has as much right to be here as I do."

John could see no reason to get upset. Besides, there was nothing he could do about it. Should a problem occur, he would take whatever steps he felt necessary at the time.

"I'm sure you remember that he's a little unstable. He always has been, but he's gotten a lot worse over the years. Did you know that he's been in the state mental hospital?" Bill asked.

"No, I didn't know that," John replied.

That bit of information caused John to think about what they were telling him a little more seriously. This put a different light on the situation. Maybe there was something in what they were saying. Maybe he should be on guard, just in case.

"Think back about twenty-five years ago. The fight you got into with him that almost kept you from going to the prom. It was over Mary Weston, wasn't it?" Bill asked.

"Yes. But what does that have to do with now? Mary isn't here."

"I don't know what it has to do with now, but he was really upset to see your name," Bill said.

"Mary was afraid of him, and I think she had reason to be," John stated flatly.

"No argument there. All I'm trying to do is warn you that he is here and for you to watch your back. You never know what he'll do," Bill warned.

Bill and Julie returned to the table, leaving John with his thoughts. It was obvious they were worried. John knew that Bill was not the type to worry needlessly. Mike wouldn't be crazy enough to start something here, or would he, John wondered.

Deep in thought, John left the meeting room and went out into the lobby. Why the hell did I agree to come to this stupid dance in the first place, he asked himself. He was thinking that this could turn out to be one of the worst times in his life. After all, he had come here to look up old school friends, not to dig up old battles he thought were long dead and buried.

John pushed the doors open and went outside.

CHAPTER FOUR

THE COOL EVENING AIR felt good on John's face. People were still coming in, but he hardly noticed them. As he walked around the courtyard, he wondered if the reason that Mary kept coming to mind was because he still loved her and still held deep feelings for her.

"Is that you, John Blake?"

His thoughts were interrupted by a woman's voice. He looked around. At first, he saw no one he knew, then he saw her. She was five foot six inches tall and carried herself well. She was a little on the heavy side, but still quite nice looking. She still had a fair figure, but it was the auburn color of her hair that gave her away. It could only be one person, Karen Carter.

"Yes, and you're Karen."

She ran to him, threw her arms around his neck and gave him a big hug. John wrapped his arms around her and hugged her back. He pulled back, took hold of her hands and held her arms out as he looked her over.

"You haven't changed much at all," he said.

He finally met someone he could relate to, someone who knew him well, even if it had been more then fifteen years since he had seen her last. She was what he needed to lift his spirits.

"Oh, I've put on a little weight and my hair has a little gray in it, but other than that I'm in pretty good shape."

"You sure are. How's life been treating you?"

"Pretty good. I met a wonderful man who thinks I'm the greatest. He's taken my two children under his wing and treats them like they were his own. I'm really very happy. What about you?"

"I'm okay. My life's had its ups and downs, but all in all I can't complain."

"Isn't anyone going to introduce me?" a nice looking older man with gray hair asked.

"I'm sorry, honey," Karen said. "John Blake this is my husband, Howard Van Scott. Howard, this is my very dear friend, John. We dated during our senior year of high school."

"Nice to meet you, John. I've heard about you from Karen. I understand you live in Colorado now."

"That's right."

"What do you do in Colorado?"

"I guess I'm what you would call retired. I decided it was time to take a little time off and visit old friends and do a little traveling. One of these days I'll probably need to find something to do, but for now I'll visit some of the old haunts."

John was surprised at his openness to a complete stranger.

"Do you have any interest in automobiles?"

"Howard, not now, please," Karen said with a tone of disgust in her voice.

"Yes, cars interest me very much."

"Tell you what, why don't you drop over for a visit before you leave the area. We can talk then," he suggested.

"Please do. Call and come have dinner with us," Karen added.

"I'll do that. I'll give you a call. Nice meeting you Howard, and it really is good to see you again, Karen."

"Save a dance for me?" Karen asked.

"Sure. I'd like that," John replied.

Karen took Howard's hand and started for the main entrance. He watched as they walked away. Karen seemed very happy and for some reason that was important to John. He wondered for a minute what Howard might have in mind, but his thoughts quickly returned to his feelings of loneliness.

JOHN STARTED WALKING AGAIN. As he walked onto a patio, he could hear the music from the band inside. The first song he heard was one he had danced to many times with Mary. Closing his eyes, he could picture Mary in his mind. He could see her as she looked when he would meet her in the hall at school every morning. He remembered how she would rush to him, throw her arms around his neck and kiss him.

The silence of his dream world was shattered by the sound of someone coming out onto the patio. He opened his eyes and looked toward the door. He saw a couple coming outside for a breath of air. They looked at him and smiled. He acknowledged seeing them with a slight nod, then went inside.

When he returned to the table, Bill and Julie were not there. They were out on the dance floor. He sat down and watched the others enjoying themselves. Shortly after the music stopped, Bill and Julie returned.

"Where have you been? We were beginning to think that you went home," Bill asked as he held out the chair for Julie.

"I went for a walk. It's a beautiful evening."

While John had been outside, Bill had gotten drinks for all of them. John sat with his elbows on the table, leaning slightly forward. His hands were wrapped around the glass in front of him. He looked at it as if he were studying the glass and its contents.

"What's the matter, John?" Julie asked. The concern in her voice showed how much Julie was worried about him. She was beginning to think that it might not have been such a good idea to have insisted that he come with them.

JOHN SLOWLY LOOKED UP from his glass. He was about to respond to Julie's question when he caught sight of three people coming into the meeting room. He froze instantly as he stared over Julie's shoulder toward the entrance to the main room.

Julie and Bill looked at him, not knowing what to think, or what might be wrong. Julie turned, looked at Bill, and then they both turned to see what it was that had caught John's attention.

A man and two women had come into the meeting room and stopped briefly to look around. John's attention was immediately drawn to the dark-haired woman who seemed to be standing back as if she did not want to be here. He held his breath as he waited for the woman to step into the light so he could see her face. He could not let himself believe that she was really here.

It was only after they started to move toward a table that the woman passed close to a light where John could see her face. He was sure it was Mary. It seemed to him that she had changed so little. There were a few small wrinkles around the corners of her mouth and eyes, but they did nothing to distract from her beauty. In fact, they made her look more mature, and even prettier than when she was a teenager.

Suddenly, John realized that something was wrong. At first he could not put his finger on it, but it soon came to him. It was her eyes. There was a sadness in his heart as he realized that her eyes did not have that sparkle. The special shine he had always enjoyed seeing was not there. Her brown eyes appeared dull and almost lifeless. He wondered what had happened to her to take the sparkle from her eyes.

Julie looked at Bill, then at John before she spoke.

"John, who's that woman? Is that Mary?"

John looked at Julie with surprise. It hadn't occurred to him until that very minute, but Julie didn't know Mary.

He looked at Bill. Like a flash of lightening, John began to realize that he was still very much in love with Mary. Even after all the years they had been apart, he still had strong feelings for her.

John watched Mary as she sat down at a table with her friends. For the first time in his life he had been afraid. He was afraid to approach her, yet afraid not to. Should he go talk to her, or should he leave her alone? What would he say to her?

"If you sit here all night looking at her, you're going to hate yourself in the morning. You'll never know if she still has any feelings for you unless you go talk to her," Bill said.

John looked at Bill. With the suddenness of a slap on the face, he realized Bill was right.

"Bill, don't push him," Julie said in disgust. "John knows what he wants and is big enough to get it in his own way, and in his own time."

"You're right, Bill," John said as he stood up. He looked at Mary, then back at Bill as he pushed his chair up to the table. He took a deep breath and started walking toward Mary.

As John walked toward her, he saw movement out of the corner of his eye. He turned his head and saw Mike Flanders. Mike was also walking toward Mary. He got there just a couple of steps before John. He heard Mike speak to Mary. He stopped and watched for Mary's reaction.

"Come dance with me," Mike said as he reached out and grabbed Mary by the wrist. His words were sharp and forceful. They were more of a command than a pleasant request.

"I don't want to dance with you," Mary said as she tried to pull herself free of his grip.

John could see that Mary was still afraid of Mike. He could see the almost terrified look in her eyes.

Tom was starting to stand up and say something to Mike, but John spoke before Tom had the chance. He spoke in a strong, firm voice.

"I think the lady made it clear that she doesn't want to dance with you. I strongly suggest you let go of her."

There was no doubt about what John would do if Mike decided not to let go of Mary. He was not as sure of what to do if Mike did let go of her. It had been a long time, and he didn't know what feelings Mary might have for him.

"Who asked you to butt in?" Mike snarled as he turned to see who had the nerve to speak to him so harshly. He knew John was around somewhere, now he knew where.

"Well, well, well, if it isn't Mary's private bodyguard. I didn't expect to see you here,"

"You knew damn well I was here."

"Why don't you just get lost before I - - -."

Mike stopped in the middle of his sentence as John took a step toward him. He instantly realized that John was still more than willing to protect Mary from him.

"Before you what?"

John was growing impatient with Mike. It was clear that he would not wait much longer for Mike to let go of Mary's wrist.

"Let go of her," John insisted.

John looked right into Mike's eyes as he inched closer.

Mike was not sure what to do. It passed through Mike's mind that John had never said anything he wasn't prepared to back up. He had challenged John in the past and had lost. Mike decided this was not the time, nor the place to challenge John again. Reluctantly, he let go of Mary's wrist but just stood there.

"I suggest you go away and leave her alone before this turns into a serious problem for you," John said firmly.

Mike's face became an angry red. He had hatred in his eyes. He looked around the room. It seemed to him that everyone was looking at him, judging him. In his mind, he was greatly outnumbered. Mike saw this as another put down in front of his classmates. It didn’t matter to Mike that only those at the table, or very close by, had any idea of what was going on. John would have to pay for it. He turned sharply and began to walk away, but stopped suddenly and turned around.

"This isn't the end of this."

Mike stared at John for a few seconds, then turned and quickly walked away.

John didn't trust Mike one bit. He waited until Mike was across the room and going out the door into the hall before he turned and looked at Mary.

MARY SAT LOOKING UP at John. The surprise of seeing him overwhelmed her. She was unable to speak or to move. She could not believe John was really there, standing only a foot or so from her. Tears filled her eyes as he reached out a hand to her. She glanced at his hand then took hold of it. In a sort of a daze, she stood up in front of him. Mary never took her eyes off John's face as she allowed him to lead her to the dance floor. She didn't know where he was leading her, but it didn't matter. She would go anywhere with him.

John turned her in front of him. Looking down at her face, he smiled and put his arm around her waist and drew her up against him. She just stood there looking up at his face in disbelief. Without any thought, she began to follow him as he slowly led her around the dance floor to the sound of the music.

It was a song they had danced to many times in the past, but it didn't matter what the music was. They were in a world of their own, oblivious to everything and everyone around them.

Mary continued to look at his face. It was a face she had seen so many times in her dreams and in her thoughts. The years had put a few lines on it, but it was a face she had always loved, and still loved. Only at this moment did she realize how much she loved him.

John's mind was full of questions. Did she really want him here? Was she the same person he remembered her to be or had the years changed her? Having her in his arms was almost too good to be true, and that caused him some apprehension.

She turned her head and laid her cheek against his shoulder. Tears rolled down her face, tears of joy and happiness. For almost twenty-five years she had missed him, now he was here.

Her mind filled with questions, too. Could this really be true? Had he really returned? Her mind was not only filled with questions, but was filled with fears. Fears that this may all be a dream. Or worse yet, that it was not a dream and he wouldn't be staying in the area. Maybe, he was just being nice to her and protecting her from Mike like he always had in the past. It has to be more than that, it just has to, she thought as she clutched his hand tightly.

John held her as if she were a scared child who needed the comfort of a strong arm. He was afraid that if he didn't hold her tight enough, she would get away from him. Yet, if he held her too tightly, he would suffocate her. He could feel the tension in her body. What was she afraid of now? Was she afraid of him?

He gently pressed his face to her hair. Her hair smelled fresh and clean, and was as soft as he had remembered. Her tears moistened his shirt where her head lay against him, but he didn't mind.

When the music stopped, John stopped moving, but continued to hold her. It was as if he were afraid to let loose of her for fear she would disappear again.

Mary stood with him, one hand on his shoulder, the other in his hand. Her head still lying on his shoulder. She could hear him breathe and hear the sound of his heartbeat. She squeezed his hand again.

Slowly, he removed his hand from the small of her back. He moved just enough to get his hand under her chin. Gently, he lifted her face so he could look into her eyes. Streaks of tears ran down her face.

"Hi," he said in a soft whisper.

A soft smile started to appear at the corners of her mouth.

"Hi," she replied in a whisper that was so soft it was almost impossible to hear.

The band began to play a fast rock and roll song from the sixties. They looked into each other's eyes.

"I don't think I'm ready for this. How about you?"

"Not yet," she replied unable to take her eyes off him.

JOHN TOOK HER BY THE HAND, as if he had a choice, and began leading her out into the hallway. She held onto him as if the minute she let go he would vanish like a puff of smoke. They walked out to the lounge near the front entrance and sat down on a couch in the corner. They could still hear the band, but it was not so loud that they would be unable to talk.

Mary sat close to him with his hand firmly clasped in hers. He took his free hand and reached into his pocket for a handkerchief. Looking into her eyes, he gently wiped the tears from her face.

John didn't know what to say to her. He had never thought this moment would ever happen. He had so many questions to ask, but he didn't know where to begin. It felt so good just to have her sitting beside him that everything else seemed insignificant.

Mary said nothing while he wiped away the tears. She had so many questions to ask him, but was a little afraid of what the answer to one of them might be. She had heard that he had married and had a couple of children. If he were still married, it would be better if she just left and never saw him again. But she was with him now and it felt good to be next to him again. She wouldn't let this moment pass. She couldn't let it pass even if he was married. She was torn between asking and being told she could no longer be near him, and not saying anything and letting what happened between them just happen, no matter what the consequences.

"How have you been?" John asked, lost for words. His eyes told her that he really wanted to know.

"I've been fine," she replied with a slight quiver in her voice.

Once again there was a long pause as they looked at one another. John decided he had to find out if she was available or if this would be the last time he would see her. Even after all these years, he felt more in love with her than he could ever remember.

"Are you - - married, or anything?" he finally asked. He felt a little foolish for putting it the way he did, but he could not think of any other way to ask.

"No," she replied.

She hesitated to ask him, but she needed to know, too.

"Are you - - married, - - or - - anything?"

John broke into a big smile. It was such a relief to get that one simple question out of the way. It was like opening a window curtain and letting the sun shine in.

"No," he replied with a sigh of relief.

The pressure of the moment was broken. It was clear that it was all right for them to once again care for each other. Their love for each other would not be tarnished by hurting someone else.

John leaned close to her, put his hand on the side of her face and gently drew her to him. Their lips met in a soft, gentle kiss. His lips pressing against the softness of her lips made his heart beat faster.

Mary reached out and put her free hand on his shoulder. It was real, he was here and he was kissing her. Her head was spinning and her heart raced with excitement. She was sure everything was going to be all right. The tension of these past weeks rapidly faded away.

John slowly leaned back and looked into her eyes. He smiled at her as he noticed that the sparkle had returned, along with a few tears.

She looked into his eyes and wondered how long he would be staying. She was almost afraid to ask, but she had to know.

"How long will you be in Michigan?" she asked.

The fear that he might be leaving soon showed in her voice.

"Well, that's hard to say. It depends on a certain lady that I care for very much, and if she wants me to stay."

Her heart almost stopped. Was that "certain lady" her, or was there someone else in his life.

John saw the worried look wash over her face and quickly realized that she was not secure enough for him to be kidding her.

"That 'certain lady', is you," he said with a gleam in his eyes that was unmistakable.

Mary let out a sigh of relief, smiled and threw her arms around his neck. She kissed him and held him tightly. She could not remember when she had been so happy. At the same time that her heart was telling her that everything was all right, her mind was trying to tell her to slow down. What if this wasn't going to work out? What if he wasn't the same gentle man she had known? What if? What if? A lot can happen to a person in twenty-five years. Maybe, she wasn't the same person he remembered her to be. Her mind kept filling her head with doubts.

John whispered in her ear, "Mary Weston, will you dance with me?"

She leaned back and looked at him. She couldn't believe that at a time like this he wanted to dance.

"We have so much to talk about."

"You're right, of course, but we have tomorrow to talk. If you want, we can spend the whole day out by the river. We can have a picnic and talk until we're hoarse. But tonight, we have the chance to dance and let the world go by without us for a little while. Besides, it also gives me a chance to hold you without everyone looking at us as if we're strange."

The tension was gone and joy was filling his heart. It had been a long time since he had felt so carefree and happy. He felt like dancing, and he wanted to hold her close.

"I would like the world to go by without us for a little while, but we are a little strange, don't you think?"

"Yes, we are. This is our first date in twenty some years, and I plan to enjoy it. So let's get off the couch and start enjoying the evening. I don't care if the whole world thinks we're crazy."

"Do you remember our first date?"

"Of course, and I plan to have as much fun on this first date as we did on our very first date," he said as he stood up and reached out his hand to her.

She looked up, smiled, then reached out and took his hand.

"You are crazy, you know that."

"Yes. I've always known that. I'm just glad you have finally found out that I'm crazy, crazy about you."

John pulled her to her feet. He put his arm around her and they walked back to the meeting room. John led Mary to the table where Bill and Julie were sitting down after finishing a dance.

John introduced Bill and Julie to Mary. Mary remembered Bill and seemed to take an immediate liking to Julie. John was pleased that Julie and Mary were getting along so well. It was important to him, as Bill and Julie were his best friends. He wanted all of them to be best friends.

The band began to play another slow song from the sixties. John looked over at Mary, and she looked at him and nodded. John stood up, then pulled Mary's chair back as she stood up. Putting his hand on the small of her back, he guided her out onto the dance floor.

Mary turned and slipped into John's arms as if it was the most natural thing in the world. With their arms around each other, Mary laid her head on his shoulder. For the first time in weeks, she felt safe and secure.

CHAPTER FIVE

MIKE FLANDERS SAT in his car in the Hoyt Meeting Center parking lot. He convinced himself that he had to do something about John before everything he had worked for was ruined.

In his mind, Mike could see John holding Mary in his arms. His anger and rage continued to build little by little until he could hardly keep it contained.

"I should be the one holding her and dancing with her, not John. He has no right to hold her. Mary belongs to me," he said as he pounded his fists against the steering wheel of his car.

Mike leaned forward and turned the ignition key to start his car. In his fury and rage, he slammed the car into reverse and backed out of the parking space, hitting the car behind him. Slamming the car into drive, it leaped forward. He turned out onto the street and pushed the gas pedal to the floor. The old car poured blue-gray smoke from the exhaust as the tires squealed leaving black streaks on the pavement.

Mike had been so sure that tonight was going to be the turning point in his otherwise dull and lonely life. But everything had suddenly changed and now he was no longer convinced that things were going his way. It had become obvious, even to him, that his plan was falling apart. The reason was obvious even to him. There was only one thing left for him to do. He had to find a way to eliminate John Blake, permanently.

Mike drove to his small apartment above Apple Annie's Vintage Clothing store in the historic district of Ypsilanti known as Depot Town. He parked in the rear of the building and used the back stairs to the third floor.

Most of the old buildings in the Historical District had been restored in an effort to bring businesses back to the area. However, Mike's apartment was still old and rundown. The wallpaper was faded and stained. The paint on the window frames and doors was cracked and peeling. Even the windows were dirty with the grime from years of neglect.

Mike entered his apartment and tossed his keys on the dresser. He sat down on the edge of the bed and buried his face in his hands. The springs creaked under his weight. He was confused, which was often the case when things didn't go the way he thought they should.

All kinds of questions came to his mind. Why did Mary still reject him? After all, John had left her to live somewhere else. What was he doing back here now? Why didn't he stay where he belonged? What do I do now?

It was the last question that was the big one for Mike. His ability to think and reason was not good. He had graduated from high school, but he was at or near the bottom of his class. He was also mentally unstable. To his way of thinking, John had become the real problem in his life, a threat to his very survival.

Mike's head was starting to ache. It always ached whenever he tried to solve a difficult problem. Whenever his head ached, he began to worry about being sent back to the state mental hospital. He didn't like it there. The dark little room they put him in had frightened him. It became a vicious circle, which caused him a great deal of pain and confusion, even to the point of causing him to black out.

In a short time, Mike felt as if his head was about to explode. He could not afford to blackout, not now. He had to figure out what to do.

On the top of Mike's dresser were several bottles of pills. He went to the dresser and retrieved a bottle that contained the strongest of the painkillers, but he had trouble getting the cap off.

Suddenly the top popped off, scattering the pills about the room. Mike got down on his hands and knees and began picking them up off the floor. While on the floor, he took two pills and put them in his mouth. He tipped his head back and swallowed them without the aid of water. He sat back against the dresser and closed his eyes, hoping that the pills would give him the quick relief he so desperately needed.

Gradually, the pills began to relieve his splitting headache, but in the process they also began to take control of him. All his fears and all his normal cautions were slipping away along with the headache until they were both completely gone. He was no longer afraid of anything or anybody. All he could think of now was how to get rid of the one person standing in his way, the one person who blocked his road to happiness.

Without John around, he could own Mary; and own her was what he wanted. He gave no thought to the fact that Mary wanted nothing to do with him, or the fact that she was still afraid of him after all those years.

Getting rid of John was Mike's number one concern, but how to do it. A number of options came to mind, but the one that came back again and again was to destroy John so that he could never interfere again.

AS TIME PASSED, some of his thought processes began to return. Now that the pain in his head was gone, he could get up off the floor. He went to the window and stood looking out, watching the street below. Across the street at Miller's Ice Cream Parlor, he saw a young couple enjoying some ice cream at one of the sidewalk tables. As he watched the couple, a plan slowly began to form in his head.

Mike left his apartment, got into his car and sat there looking out the windshield for several minutes. He had but one thing on his mind. Without any conscious thought, he started the car and drove down the alley. He turned through the parking lot and out onto Cross Street. He drove across

River Street, across the railroad tracks and into the alley behind the old Thompson Building, less than two blocks from his apartment.

Parking his car, he got out and looked around to see if anyone was watching him. He saw no one. He unlocked the door, opened it and quickly stepped inside, shutting the door behind him. He looked through a very small window to see if anyone had seen him enter the building. After all, this was his secret hiding place.

Mike often needed a place like this, a place where he felt safe and secure. He spent a lot of time here. In this large secure room, Mike could feel strong and important, something he never felt in the outside world. It was also a place where his personal things would be safe from prying eyes and nosey landlords.

One corner of the room was arranged like a small lounge. There was a large overstuffed chair that had seen better days. The stuffing was pushing out of several holes in the arms and back. The large sofa was old and covered in a dingy green vinyl. It was greasy and showed signs of years of wear. The coffee table was marred and beat up. It was dirty and had rings from wet glasses that had been set on it. There were several Playboy and Hustler magazines on it, and an ashtray that was full of wrappers from cupcakes, cookies and candy bars.

Along one wall was a large gray steel locker. It stood about six feet tall and was four feet wide with two doors. It looked out of place in the dingy room, because it was the only thing in the entire room that appeared to be neat and clean.

Mike stood in front of the locker, looking at it. It was as if he wasn't sure if he should open it. Finally, he put the key in the lock, unlocked the door and opened the locker.

On the inside of one door, he had pictures of Playboy centerfolds. On the inside of the other door, he had a piece of white cloth. The cloth had been cut with a great deal of care to fit over the inside of the door perfectly.

The right side of the locker was all shelves that held stacks of magazines and paperback books. On the upper shelf there was several boxes of ammunition, some for pistols, some for rifles and shotguns. Along side the ammunition were two pistols. One was a large .45 caliber revolver, the other a smaller 9mm automatic. Mike picked up the smaller pistol and tucked it in his belt.

In the left side of the locker were two rather large caliber rifles, one small .22 caliber rifle with a scope and two twelve-gauge shotguns. Mike looked at the rifles for a long time. He had to make the right choice. Even though Mike had a very hard time thinking things out, he seemed to understand that John was the only one he really wanted to hurt.

Although Mike had several guns, he had little opportunity to practice with any of them. The only one that he had done any amount of shooting with was the .22 caliber rifle. It was the only one he had any real confidence in using with a good degree of accuracy.

He picked up the .22 caliber rifle with the scope and set it down on the sofa. He unlocked the back door and looked out. He looked up at the window of the house across the alley. There were no lights on in the house and he could see no one around.

Mike took all of the guns out of the cabinet. He put them in the back of his station wagon and covered them with a dirty old Army blanket he had purchased at an Army Surplus Store.

After taking several boxes of ammunition from the locker, he closed and locked it. He took the .22 caliber rifle out to the car and put it on the floor behind the front seat then got in his car.

MIKE DROVE BACK TO THE Hoyt Meeting Center parking lot. He parked his car and then sat looking toward the meeting center as he tried to figure out a way to destroy John without hurting anyone else. In his drug-induced state, his mind told him that if anyone else got hurt, everyone would be after him. But no one would care, or even miss John.

The pills he had taken earlier were beginning to lose some of their effectiveness. Mike's headache was beginning to return. It was only a dull ache at the moment, but he knew it would get worse if he didn't take more pills. He wanted more pills, but in his rush to get back to the meeting center, he had left them in his room. There was no time to go back because he knew where John could be found now. He had no idea where John was staying or how long he would be in the area. If he was going to rid himself of John's interference, he had to do it now, tonight.

Mike looked around the grounds. He needed a place where he could get a good view of the doors to the Hoyt Meeting Center. From where he was sitting, he could see only the door to the patio that overlooked the river. It seemed to be the place where people came out to get a breath of air. He remembered that there was a door with another patio located on the side of the building. He looked around for a place where he might be able to see both patios at the same time. There was a small grove of trees across the drive. If he could get over there without being seen, he would be able to see both doors and patios.

Being careful not to be seen, Mike got out of the car and took the rifle from the back seat. Holding the rifle down close to his leg, he walked across the parking lot and into the dark shadows of the trees.

Even with his head hurting more and more with each passing minute, Mike realized he would have to have some way to get away. He looked from the patio toward the river. He noticed that the cover provided by the small grove of trees would keep him from being seen for only a short distance. Once he was out of the trees, it would be wide open all the way down the sloping lawn to Huron River Drive.

Even though he would be in the open, he would be far enough away from the Hoyt Meeting Center that no one would be able to recognize him. From Huron River Drive, he could across the street to McDonald's and run around back. From the back of McDonald's parking lot, he could go down the embankment to the railroad tracks. After that, he should be home free. From there, he could go any direction he wanted without being seen.

Mike began working his way among the trees. He soon found a tree that branched out forming a V between its main branches. Moving in under the tree, he worked himself into a position where he could see both of the patios clearly. He rested his rifle in between the branches of the tree and waited.

Mike could hear music coming from inside the hall. He watched as a couple came out onto the patio. He positioned his rifle, using the man to sight in on. Mike smiled to himself as he looked through the scope at the man. This was going to be an easy shot, he thought. All he had to do was to wait for John and Mary to come out onto one of the patios.

Suddenly, a thought passed through his head. What if they don't come out onto one of the patio? What if they leave by the front door without ever coming out here? What if they have already left the dance?

The pain in his head was slowly getting worse as the thought of all the things that could go wrong with his plan began to clutter his mind. The effects of his medication were wearing off and he began to feel nervous, even a little frightened. Maybe, someone walking past would discover him before he had a chance to do what he was here to do.

His head began to throb. The pain was becoming almost unbearable. His head hurt so much that his vision was becoming blurred. He shook his head and rubbed his temples in an attempt to relieve some of the pain.

Mike looked up toward the patios. The first couple he had seen on the patio had gone back inside. Now another couple was coming out. He hoped it would be John and Mary. He didn't know how much longer he could stand the pain in his head and still do what his clouded mind knew had to be done.

MARY AND JOHN SPENT the evening dancing to the songs they had danced to in their youth. Although they did enjoy a few fast dances, they preferred the slow ones, the ones that allowed them to be in each other's arms.

Mary couldn't let go of John's hand for more then a second or two at a time. She had found him, and this time she was not going to let him get away. It was still hard for her to believe that she was with him again after all those years.

John didn't mind having Mary hang onto him. It simply reassured him that she loved him. He was rapidly discovering that the love he had for her was still there and as strong as ever, maybe stronger.

During the breaks, Mary and John spent time getting reacquainted with a few old friends. Tomorrow they could talk about the past and plan for the future. Tonight was a time to celebrate their reunion.

Karen Van Scott and her husband joined John and Mary for a drink. They talked about their high school days. Although Howard didn't know Mary and John at that time, he seemed to understand what was happening to them this evening.

After a short visit with Karen and Howard, John stood up and reached out to Mary. She took his hand and let him lead her back to the dance floor. She slipped into his arms once again and they began moving to the rhythm of the music. She felt at peace with herself and with the rest of the world, a feeling she had not felt for many years. The fears and frustrations of the past several weeks seemed to fade away.

The music stopped, but Mary didn't want it to stop. She wanted to stay in John's arms. Still holding onto him, she looked up and smiled. John leaned down and gave her a kiss.

"Let's go outside for a minute," John suggested.

Mary smiled and went with him to the patio. Another couple was just coming in as they went out. Mary stepped up to the steel railing to look out over the well kept lawn toward the river. John moved up behind her and wrapped his arms around her. She leaned back against him, putting her hands over his. She closed her eyes to savor this moment. It had been a long time since she had been held.

"The moon is sure bright. Look at the shadows of the trees on the lawn," John said in a whisper.

"It's a beautiful evening," Mary sighed.

John squeezed her gently in his arms. It felt very comforting to have her leaning back against his chest. He nestled his face in her soft hair and smelled the delicate fragrance.

Mary could feel his breath in her hair and on her neck. She held his arms around her as if to let go of him would end the evening. She felt cozy and protected in his arms. She wanted to keep these feelings forever.

"I love you," John whispered in her ear.

"I love you, too," she replied softly.

MIKE WATCHED AS JOHN and Mary came out onto the patio. He didn't like John holding Mary so closely. Although Mike could not hear them, he could tell that John was winning her away from him. Anger built up inside him like a raging forest fire, growing hotter and hotter with each passing second.

The pain in his head continued to become almost unbearable. His head was hurting him so much that he could hardly see. If he was going to destroy John, he had to do it now.

He lifted the rifle to his shoulder and pointed it at John. With the pain pounding in his head, it was hard for him to hold the rifle steady and to focus on his target. He couldn't allow himself to miss his target. Yet, he could not wait much longer, either. The fear that he might blackout before he got his shot off was weighing heavily on his mind.

JOHN SLID HIS ARMS from around Mary and stepped up beside her. She turned around and stepped in front of him. Reaching up, she put her arms around his neck. John wrapped his arms around her narrow waist and gently pulled her up against him. She looked up at him. The love she had for him showed on her face and in the sparkle in her eyes. He leaned down to kiss her.

Suddenly, there was a loud crack in the air. Mary's body suddenly jerked against him. Her eyes opened wide with surprise. A shocked look quickly spread over Mary's face as she stared up at John. It was as if she was pleading for help, but she said nothing.

It took a second for John to realize that something was terribly wrong. It took another second or two for it to register in his mind that Mary had been shot.

Mary's eyes slowly began to close as shock took hold of her. She laid her head down on John's chest as her knees buckled and her legs gave way. Slowly, she began to slide down him. John held her tightly as he lowered her to the patio deck. He crouched over her to protect her from any further harm. The sudden realization of what was happening hit John hard.

"God, NO, not now," he pleaded.

Bill and Julie were on their way out to the patio and saw Mary go limp in John's arms. Bill had also heard the rifle shot. He pushed Julie back inside the hallway, then ran to help John. Bill turned and looked toward the door.

"Call for an ambulance and the police," he yelled to Julie.

Julie couldn't believe what was happening. She stood there with her hands over her mouth, and her eyes wide in disbelief.

"NOW!" Bill yelled.

Julie quickly recovered, realizing that she was needed. She turned and ran to the lobby to call for help.

While Bill was kneeling down beside John, someone grabbed a tablecloth and rushed it out to Bill. John was holding Mary in his arms. She was breathing, but it was becoming gradually more labored as the seconds ticked by. Bill helped John wrapped Mary in the tablecloth. John looked up at Bill. The fear of losing her was clearly written across John's face. Bill tried to reassure John that everything would be all right, but it was far from what he felt.

"Help is on the way, John. Just keep her still and hold her."

John felt so helpless. He didn't have to be told to hold on to her. He held her in his arms, but he was sure he could feel her slipping away. He couldn't let her slip away, not now, not after he had just found her again.

John could hear the sound of the sirens as they grew closer. The police arrived just minutes before the ambulance. They immediately moved all the onlookers back into the hall, then began to check the grounds to make sure it was safe.

"Please, Mary, hold on. They'll be here soon," John pleaded.

It wasn't long before the paramedics arrived, but to John it seemed like it took forever. He hesitated to release Mary to the paramedics, but something in his mind told him to move aside to allow them to do their job.

He stood by helplessly as he watched a paramedic start an IV while another took Mary's blood pressure. The paramedics worked very fast and efficiently. They had Mary ready to move to the hospital in a matter of minutes.

Mary was carefully lifted onto the stretcher. As they rolled the stretcher toward the ambulance, John followed alongside.

"I'm going with her," John declared.

"We'll meet you at the hospital in a little while," Bill called out.

As they put Mary in the ambulance, John climbed in the back and sat down next to her. The doors were closed and within seconds the ambulance was speeding down the street toward the hospital.

John watched as the paramedics put an oxygen mask over Mary's face and started a second IV. Her breathing was labored and raspy, she seemed so pale.

John felt so helpless. He reached out and touched her fingertips with his. He prayed as he had never prayed before.

CHAPTER SIX

THE SOUND OF THE RIFLE shot came as a surprise to everyone, even to Mike. He didn't realize that he had actually pulled the trigger. Everything was a blur. His head was splitting with pain, and the pain was making him feel strange. It was as if someone, or something was controlling him.

Mike looked over the top of the rifle and could see all the confusion on the patio. It took a few seconds for him to realize that he had done what he came here to do. A feeling of joy spread through him, a feeling he rarely had the opportunity to experience during his entire life. It seemed that he had always been a failure, but tonight he was sure that he had succeeded.

He lifted the rifle up and looked through the scope in an effort to see what he had done, to savor his accomplishment if only for a moment. He suddenly realized that something was wrong, very wrong.

Fear began to grip him as his mind slowly let him understand what he was seeing. There had been only two people on the patio when he pulled the trigger. Now there were three and more were coming. He could see John hovering over Mary behind the steel railing. John seemed to be protecting her.

Slowly it began to sink into his clouded and confused mind that he had shot Mary. Mike couldn't believe what he had done. He backed away from the tree in a growing state of panic. His feeling of joy quickly changed to feelings of fear.

As he turned to run, he dropped the rifle on the ground. He ran wildly through the trees and across the open lawn as if the devil himself was after him. He ran across the road, through the McDonald's parking lot and down the embankment toward the railroad tracks.

His fear was so great, and the pain in his head so severe, that he didn't feel the sharp thorns of the berry bushes and the heavy cattails as they poked and slapped at him. The thorny bushes tore at his clothes and skin as he tried to run through the thick undergrowth.

He had no idea where he was going. The pounding pain in his head wouldn't allow him to think. He ran as if his life depended on it, running head long into a grove of Hawthorn bushes. Their long, hard pointed needle-like stickers stabbed and pricked him relentlessly as he tried to push his way through to the railroad tracks.

Suddenly, everything seemed to be going blank. The ground seemed to be coming up to him in slow motion as he fell into the Hawthorn bushes. It registered in his mind that he was falling, but he didn't feel anything, nor could he stop himself. As soon as he collapsed on the ground, everything went black.

SHORTLY AFTER THE AMBULANCE left for the hospital, Lieutenant Palmer arrived on the scene. He quickly took control of the investigation and began searching the area for clues. Within a few minutes, one of the police officers had found the rifle lying near a tree.

"Lieutenant Palmer, I found the weapon," the officer called out.

"Don't touch it," Lieutenant Palmer said as he started toward the grove of trees where the officer was standing.

When he reached the small grove of trees, he looked around. The small grove of trees would have provided the shooter with good cover and good support for his rifle.

The grass on one side of the base of the tree had been stomped down which would indicate that the shooter had been waiting there for a period of time. It had been a good location to shoot from if the intended target was on the patio.

With the evidence that Palmer had at the site led him to believe that Mary had been shot from the small grove of trees. However, there was one problem. The only logical escape route was wide open offering very little protection for perpetrator's escape.

Lieutenant Palmer looked around at the ground. He continued to look from the trees to the porch where Mary was shot and back on down the slopping lawn toward McDonald's. He had no evidence to support his thoughts, but he was convinced of two things. First of all, he didn't believe that the evidence supported it as a random shooting. The shooter had been waiting too long for it to be considered a random shooting. Secondly, since the escape route was a poor choice, the shooting was done by an amateur.

Lieutenant Palmer picked up the rifle with care. There was little doubt in his mind that it was the gun used in the shooting.

"I want pictures taken of this area and of the patio from here. I also want you to gather together all the people in the meeting room and start asking them what they know about this. I want to know what they heard, what the saw, and any ideas they might have as to who might have done this," Lieutenant Palmer instructed the sergeant.

"Whoever did the shooting must have had a reason. From the looks of this place he must have been here for a while."

"How do you know that?"

Lieutenant Palmer turned around to see who was asking him questions.

"Who are you?" Lieutenant Palmer asked.

"I'm Bill Jordan. For your information, the woman who was shot is Mary Weston. She was on the patio with her long time friend, John Blake. My wife and I were just on our way outside when the shot was fired."

"Did you see who fired the shot?"

"First, answer my question."

Lieutenant Palmer looked at Bill for a moment. He wasn't sure that he wanted to answer his question, but decided that it wouldn't do any harm to his investigation.

"Whoever it was had been here for awhile. I know that because of the amount of grass that has been trampled down on just one side of this tree, the side away from the balcony. Now answer my questions."

"No. I didn't see who fired the shot, but it came from here. I saw a small muzzle flash just as I opened the door to the patio. I didn't see anyone. I was far too concerned with Mary and John to be looking down here."

"Where is this John Blake now?"

"He's --." Bill started to answer Lieutenant Palmer's question, but was interrupted.

An officer came running up the hill.

"Lieutenant Palmer, we have a witness at McDonald's who said he saw a man running from up here, down past McDonald's and into the brush along the railroad tracks."

"Get some help down there and see if you can pick up a trail," Lieutenant Palmer ordered.

"I'd be very careful going into that brush."

"Why? What's in there, Mr. Jordan?" Lieutenant Palmer asked.

"That place is full of Hawthorns and berry bushes," Bill advised. "I'd send someone down near the paper mill, maybe on the bridge so he could see anyone crossing LeForge Road on either side of the river. There is almost nowhere else to go except back here or along the tracks toward Ann Arbor, unless, of course, whoever it was likes to swim."

Lieutenant Palmer looked at Bill for a second, then gave the order.

"Send someone to the LeForge Road bridge and have them keep an eye on both sides of the bridge. Send a unit down to Superior Road to watch the track in case he might go that way."

Turning back to Bill, he asked him again, “Now, where did you say this John Blake can be found?"

"He can be found at the hospital. He left in the ambulance with Miss Weston."

"Since you seem to know so much, maybe you know why someone might have wanted to shoot, - ah, - Mary Weston?"

"I don't know any reason why anyone would want to shoot Mary. She just returned from South America after living there for over twenty years. I personally think she was mistaken for someone else."

"You may be right," Lieutenant Palmer said.

He took a second to look toward the balcony. Bill could be right, he thought. It would be easy to mistake someone for someone else in this light, even with a scope.

"I might want to talk to you later. Where will I be able to find you?"

"My wife and I are going over to the hospital. John has been staying with us. We need to find out how Mary's doing."

Bill had said all he was going to say for the moment. He had some questions of his own, but he needed time to sort them out.

Bill turned and headed back up to the patio where Julie was waiting for him. He grabbed Julie's arm and quickly led her off the patio toward the parking lot.

"Where are we going?" Julie asked.

"To the hospital. Something strange is going on here."

Julie had to almost run to keep up with Bill. She got in the car and waited until they were on their way to the hospital before she asked him any more questions.

"What did you mean when you said 'something strange is going on'?" She was afraid Bill had heard something while he was talking to the police.

"I don't know, but I do know it doesn't make sense. Something only a nut case could come up with," Bill replied while deep in thought.

Julie looked at him as he drove. She sat quietly, thinking about what had happened, and what Bill had said. The term "nut case" stuck in her mind. It made her immediately think of Flanders and the way he acted when he saw John was at the reunion.

THE MOOM WAS HIGH overhead when Mike woke up. He felt cold and damp. It took him a few minutes to clear his head enough to remember where he was and how he had gotten there. As his senses returned, he realized he had not been unconscious for very long.

Although his head didn't hurt as much as it did when he fired his rifle, he could feel pain over most of his body. Running his hands over his face, he wiped at the moisture that was running down his cheeks. It felt sticky. Mike looked at his hands and could see a dark color in the moonlight. His face began to sting from the sweat from his hands. He quickly realized his face was covered with small cuts and scratches.

He started to move, but was immediately stuck in the back of the neck by a Hawthorn spine. He jerked away and let out a soft cry of pain as another thorn stuck him in the back. Mike put his hand over his mouth. He was afraid that someone might hear him. Mike lay quietly and listened, but didn't hear anyone coming. Slowly, he crawled out from under the Hawthorn bushes and stood up beside the railroad tracks.

Stopping to look back toward the Hoyt Meeting Center, he could see red and blue flashing lights. He also saw someone coming out of the shadows of the trees holding something in his hand. It was his rifle.

It had not taken the police long to find his rifle. Mike was sure it wouldn't take them long to find him if he didn't get moving. He reached down to his belt for the pistol he had been carrying, but it was gone. He realized that he had probably lost it while running threw the bushes. It would be hard to find in the dark. With the police starting to search for him, he could not risk going back to look for it.

Mike took a quick look up and down the railroad tracks. He was not sure which direction he should go. If he followed the railroad tracks to the railroad depot, he would be right behind his apartment. He would be able to get to his pills in a relatively short time. The only problem was that the tracks were in clear view of LeForge Road for several hundred yards in both directions.

The other direction offered him didn't seem to be any better a solution. If he went the other way, he would be going toward Ann Arbor. That would take him farther away from his pills, and farther away from a safe place to hide.

Mike decided he would be better off trying to make it across LeForge Road, than to remain on the streets of the city by circling around. The police were still not very well organized for a search. The longer he hesitated, the more time the police would have to get organized, and the greater his risk of getting caught.

Mike started along the railroad tracks toward the old paper mill and dam. As he got closer to LeForge Road, he noticed something shining just on the other side of the road. What he saw was the streetlight reflecting off the light bar on top of a police car, and two policemen were getting out of the car.

Mike ducked into the brush and crouched down in the shadows to watch. He needed time to think, to decide what to do. One of the policemen walked up the road and stood near a light pole while the other officer walked toward the bridge. Mike guessed that one officer was going across the bridge to keep watch from the other side.

Mike quickly realized that the police had sealed off his escape across LeForge Road. Looking back the other direction, he saw a number of flashing lights in the McDonald's parking lot. Going toward Ann Arbor was out of the question now.

He was beginning to feel trapped. The stress was causing his head to start pounding again. He had to make a decision before his head hurt so much he would be unable to think at all.

Mike began to realize his only hope was to get in the water and swim across to the other side. From there he could go around the old paper mill and slip back into the water below the dam. If he was careful and stayed close to the brush along the shore, he might be able to wade under the bridge and on down the river to safety.

He carefully worked his way through the bushes to the river. Mike was not a very good swimmer, but he had no choice. There was a string of buoys strung across in front of the dam. They would provide him with something to hang onto as he crossed. He lowered himself into the cool water, took hold of the rope attached to the buoys and began pulling himself across the river.

The cool water felt good. It helped wash the blood from his face and clean his wounds. It also helped relieve some of the pressure he was feeling from his headache. It reminded him of the cool wet cloths his mother would put on his forehead when he was a child. He could not remember a time in his life when he didn't have headaches during times of stress. They had only gotten worse as he grew older.

Pulling himself hand over hand on the rope, he made it across the river. As soon as his feet touched the bottom again, he crawled out of the water. He worked his way around the old mill house, staying up against the building. When he reached the back of the building, he sat down and slide down the side of the dam along the bank of the river until he was back in the water. The current was fast below the dam, but the water was shallow.

The moonlight gave him enough light to see his way along the edge of the river. It also cast shadows from the trees and shrubs along the river bank. Mike crouched in the shadows as he waded down the river staying close to the bank. He was able to get past the police by passing under the bridge. It gave him a degree of satisfaction to think that he had outsmarted them. Once he was sure that he could not be seen, he stood up, but he continued on down the river staying in the water.

The cool night air and the confidence he was feeling at the moment, made the pain in his head more tolerable, at least for now. Each bridge he came to, he would slowly work his way past by moving among the shadows along the bank and under the bridge.

When he got to Frog Island, he knew he was close to Depot Town. Mike waded past the island and under the Cross Street Bridge. He came out of the river into Riverside Park at the Tridge, a Y shaped bridge crossing the river in three different directions.

He looked around and found the park was empty. He was feeling a bit chilled due to the cool night air and his wet clothes. His head was aching a little, but he could stand it for a little while longer. He walked across the Tridge to the other side of the river, then into a nearby alley.

Mike was about to step out of the alley when he saw a police car slowly cruising the street. The police officer was shining his spotlight into dark corners, between buildings and into alleys. Mike ducked down behind a dumpster and hid among some discarded boxes. He laid very still as the beam of light from the spotlight passed over him. His anxiety was causing his head to throb again.

As soon as the police car was gone, Mike ran across the street into another alley. If he was careful, he could work his way back to his apartment without being seen. Mike stayed close to the buildings, ducking into doorways and behind dumpsters.

Suddenly, Mike remembered that he had left his car in the parking lot of the Hoyt Meeting Center. It would not be long before all the people at the dance would be gone. That would leave only his car in the parking lot. The police were sure to check it out. It would not take long before they would know who he was, and within minutes they would know where he lived. Maybe, he would get lucky and they would think the car was left because the driver was too drunk to drive and got a ride with someone else, or called a cab.

There were just too many loose ends for Mike to be able to cope. His headache was getting worse again. He ran down the alley to the staircase that led up the back of the building to his apartment. He had to hurry. He had to get to his pills before the police found out where he lived, and before the pain got so great that he would pass out.

In his haste, he missed a step and slipped on the stairs, twisting his ankle and banging his shin against the edge of a step. A shooting pain shot from his ankle up his leg as he fell forward onto the second floor landing. Just as he sat up, the lights of a car turned into the alley. He quickly laid down and rolled up against the wall. He laid still knowing that he could not run.

The car moved slowly along the alley. It was another police car. He watched through an opening in the rail as the car moved past. He could hardly breathe, he hardly dared to breathe.

After the police car turned the corner, he sat up. He rubbed his ankle in an effort to reduce the pain. Using the rail for support, he stood up. It was painful to put his weight on the ankle, but he could not stay there. He had to get to his apartment to get dry clothes, but most of all he had to get to his pills.

Once he made it to his apartment, he let himself in, then locked the door behind him. He got out of his wet clothes and slipped into a pair of shorts. He took two of his pills, then laid back on his bed and closed his eyes. The medication took effect quickly. Within a few minutes he was fast asleep.

CHAPTER SEVEN

THE PARAMEDIC CONTINUALLY monitored Mary's vital signs until they arrived at the hospital. She was rushed into an emergency room. John tried to follow, but was quickly stopped by a nurse.

"I'm sorry, sir, you can't go in there," she said with a strong note of authority. "She will get the best care possible. Why don't you come and sit down?"

John nodded in response and followed the nurse to a waiting room. He began to pace back and forth, and wandered around the room while he waited for the nurse to return. When she returned, she had a cup of coffee and a clipboard with a form on it.

"I thought you might like this," she said with a smile as she handed John the coffee. "The doctor will be in to see you shortly."

"Thank you."

"I'm sorry, but I'll need to get some information. What is her name?" the nurse asked.

"Mary Weston," John replied, not paying much attention to the nurse. He was too concerned about Mary to be interested in a bunch of questions.

"Mr. Weston, is she allergic to anything that you know of?"

Calling him “Mr. Weston” startled John for a second. He turned and looked at the nurse. It wasn’t so much what she had called him as it was the sudden realization that he didn't know some of the more intimate details of Mary's life. He didn't know if she was allergic to anything, what illnesses she might have had, not even her blood type. It had never occurred to him that this information would be important, but then why would he know it. He had not seen her for over twenty years.

"I'm sorry, I don't know. I'm not Mr. Weston. She's not married. I'm John Blake, her very close friend."

The nurse apologized for her assuming they were married, but continued to ask the required questions writing down as many as John was able to answer. John answered as many as he could which were very few. Since there was no one else to speak for Mary, John signed the forms. As he finished signing, the doctor came into the waiting room.

"I'm Doctor Mathers," he said as he approached John.

"How is she doing, doctor?" John asked. His concern showed in his face as well as in his voice.

"We have your wife stabilized. However, we are going to have to take her to surgery. The bullet entered her back between her ribs. We don't think it punctured her lungs, but it does appear to be lodged against them. We are going to remove the bullet and repair any damage that may have been done."

Doctor Mathers was very professional in his manner and hoped John understood him. He was also trying not to worry John any more than necessary.

"Will she be all right?" John asked, fearing the worst.

"We are fortunate in that it doesn't look like much internal damage was done. It appears to be a very small caliber bullet. I would think that she should be all right," the doctor reassured him. "The surgery will take at least an hour. If I don't get back to you soon, please try not to worry too much."

"Thank you. Can I see her before she goes into surgery?"

"Yes, but it will be in a couple of minutes. I'll send a nurse out as soon as you can see her."

Doctor Mathers turned and disappeared into another room.

John took a sip of the coffee and sat down to wait. Waiting had always been hard for him, but somehow this seemed to be the longest 'couple of minutes' wait he had ever experienced. His mind was so consumed with his concern for Mary's well-being that he didn't even think about why someone would shoot her.

"Mr. Blake, you can see her now. Please make it brief. The doctor will be ready for her in a few minutes," the nurse advised him.

John followed the nurse into the emergency room. Mary was lying on her side on a gurney with her eyes closed. She appeared pale and weak. It scared John to see her like that. He walked up to her, took her hand in his and gently squeezed it.

"I love you," he whispered.

John was sure he felt her squeeze his hand ever so slightly. He just stood there looking at her. Her breathing seemed to be a little less labored. He looked up as two attendants entered the room with the nurse.

"The doctor's ready," the nurse said. "You can wait in the waiting room."

Reluctantly, John let go of Mary's hand. He watched as the attendants wheeled her out of the room. He followed them as far as he could, then watched as she disappeared behind the doors into the operating room. There was nothing else for him to do, except wait and pray.

JOHN WAS PACING THE FLOOR of the waiting room when Bill and Julie arrived. Julie's heart went out to him. He looked so tired, so worried and scared. She went to him and took hold of his hand in an effort to provide what little comfort she could.

"How is Mary?" she asked.

"She's in surgery right now. The doctor said he thought she will be okay, but you know anything can happen."

Julie squeezed his hand lightly. She knew there was nothing she could do to make this time easier for him.

"She'll be okay," Bill added, trying to reassure him. Deep down, Bill was as worried as John was. He knew how much Mary meant to his best friend.

"Come sit down, John. We'll wait with you," Julie said.

John followed her to the sofa and sat down beside her. Holding his hand, she could feel the tension that had built up in him. She looked across the room at Bill. The look on Julie's face told Bill that she could feel the inner pain John was experiencing.

The three of them waited in silence for word of Mary's condition. Time seemed to stand still. Everyone's head turned toward the door at the sound of footsteps in the hall. The apprehension that filled the room was overwhelming. It was a disappointment to all of them when Lieutenant Palmer came through the door.

"Mr. John Blake?" he asked looking directly at John.

"Yes?"

"I'm Lieutenant Palmer. I'm sorry to disturb you at a time like this, but I do need to ask you some questions."

"I understand."

John did understand, although he didn't feel much like talking to the police.

"Thank you. What is your relationship to Miss Weston?"

Lieutenant Palmer felt a little uncomfortable having to ask questions at this time, but it was his job. The only thing that made it easier for him was that he knew the more information he had, and the quicker he got that information, the better his chances of catching the person who committed the crime. The longer he waited to ask these questions, the less likely he was to get good clear information.

"She is a very good friend," John replied simply. It was almost as if it was what he was supposed to say. Deep down in his heart he knew that she was far more than a good friend to him.

"Can you tell me what happened?"

"I really don't know."

"Please tell me what you do know."

"We were standing on the patio at Hoyt Meeting Center when I heard a shot. Mary went limp in my arms," John told him as he relived that frightful moment.

"I see. Can you think of anyone who would have a reason to shoot Miss Weston?"

"No. Mary's been out of the country for over twenty years. I don't think she's been back more than a few weeks, maybe a month. Tonight was the first time that we've seen each other since high school," John said, his voice showing that he still was having a hard time understanding why anyone would shoot her.

"Well, this has got me baffled. We have a woman who's been out of the country for over twenty years, and who was shot for no apparent reason. I don't understand. It would have to be some strange kind of person to just shoot someone at random. That means we have a real nut out there," Lieutenant Palmer said as he thought out loud.

Bill looked over at Julie. The expression on his face told her what he was thinking.

"Lieutenant Palmer, this may be a long shot, but I think there is someone you might want to question."

John looked at Bill. He wondered what Bill could be thinking. Lieutenant Palmer looked curious, too.

"What's on you mind, Mr. Jordan?"

"Well, like I said it may be a long shot, but it's a place to start. At the dance this evening, Mike Flanders was trying to get Mary to dance with him. She refused, but he was not about to take 'no' for an answer. He was trying to force Mary to dance with him when John told him to leave her alone. They had a few words and then Mike left.

“Mike went away very angry. At the time I didn't think it was anything too serious, but I'm not so sure anymore."

"When Mike came into the dance to sign in and saw John’s name, his face got red. You could see the anger in his eyes. He was apparently very upset to find John was at the Class Reunion. I got the impression that Mike was actually shocked to see that John was there," Julie added as she looked at Lieutenant Palmer.

"It might help for you to know that Mike and John have never gotten along,” Bill added. “In fact, I think it would be fair to say that Mike hates John. Mike had a terrible crush on Mary back in high school, but Mary would have nothing to do with him. She was always afraid of Mike, and John was always there to protect her from him, just like tonight."

"You mean this whole thing goes back more than twenty years?" Lieutenant Palmer asked.

The tone of his voice showed that he found it hard to believe. He had known people who had held a grudge, but this wasn't normal.

"I’m not saying this is the case,” Bill replied. “I'm just suggesting it as a possibility."

"Like you said, 'It's a place to start'," Lieutenant Palmer said after giving it some thought. "It gives me a suspect. That's a lot more than I had when I got here."

"I don't think Mike would shoot Mary. It doesn't make any sense," John said.

"I don't think he would, either. I think he was trying to shoot you," Bill said flatly.

John just looked at him. Bill had never been one for beating around the bush and tonight was certainly no exception. When he had something to say, he said it. John had to think about that idea for a minute. There was no doubt in anyone's mind that Mike hated John, but to shoot at him was something else.

"Lieutenant, it might be important for you to know that Mike Flanders was in the state mental hospital about two, maybe three years ago, but I don’t know for how long. I don't know all the facts, but you might find it interesting to look into," Bill suggested.

"That's good to know. I'll have him picked up. I think it would be a good idea to have a little talk with him.

“What Mr. Jordan says just might make some sense, Mr. Blake. I'm going to put a police watch on you and Miss Weston. If he's crazy enough to try to shoot you at a dance where there are a lot of people around, he may be crazy enough to try it again. I'll get back to you as soon as I can."

Lieutenant Palmer said goodnight to everyone, then left. This whole thing was beginning to look like he was dealing with a real psycho, and a hate-jealousy-love triangle that had been going on for over twenty years.

Kay and Tom Sinclair came into the waiting room just as Lieutenant Palmer was leaving. Kay walked up to John and put her arms around him, giving him a hug.

"Sorry we're so late getting here. How is Mary?"

"We don't know yet. She's still in surgery," John replied.

"Is there anything we can do?" Tom asked Julie.

"Just pray," Julie replied.

"Bill, do you really think that Mike did this?" John asked.

"I don't know, but can you think of anyone else who dislikes you as much as he does, and is crazy enough to do something like this?" Bill argued.

"We told you how he looked when he saw you were at the dance. I saw his eyes. I believe he could do it. But I think Bill's right, I don't think he meant to hurt Mary at all," Julie interjected. "I think Mike was out to kill you."

"Are you referring to Mike Flanders?" Kay asked, somewhat surprised at the mention of Mike's name.

Was it possible that Mike had been the one scaring Mary all along? Kay wanted to tell the others about what had been happening to Mary before she came to stay with them, but thought it best not to say anything in front of John right now. He had enough to deal with and didn't need this to upset him even more.

"I find this whole thing crazy," John said in frustration.

John tried to put everything that had happened into some kind of logical order, something that would make sense. He was so deep in thought that he didn't hear the doctor come into the room.

"MR. BLAKE, MISS WESTON is out of surgery. She will be just fine," Doctor Mathers said

"Can I see her?"

"In a minute. Miss Weston will be able to be up and around by tomorrow. Does she have someone she can stay with after she's discharged?" he asked.

"Yes, of course. She can stay with us," Kay replied.

"She was not hurt as badly as we first thought, but she will need rest and quiet for a few days. The bullet bruised one of her ribs and the membrane, or sac, around the lungs.

"We got the bullet out without any problems, but she will have some discomfort every time she breathes because of the nature of the bruises. She will need to take it easy for several days after we release her," the doctor explained.

"When will she be able to get out of the hospital?" John asked.

"Probably, - - I'd say Tuesday, maybe Wednesday, if there's no complications. I don't really expect any. She seems to be in pretty good health. She won't be doing anything strenuous for a while, though. I will want her back in my office to remove the stitches in about a week."

"Thanks, doctor," John said.

"You can go see her now, but she will probably be too sleepy to know you're there."

John looked at the others. They seemed as relieved about Mary as he was.

"You go ahead. We'll wait for you. We can visit her tomorrow," Julie said.

"Thanks," he said as Julie gave him a hug.

John followed the doctor down the hall to the recovery room. The doctor simply pointed toward the bed where Mary lay. John went to the side of the bed, leaned down and kissed her on the forehead. She seemed to have regained some of her color, but still looked very frail and weak. He reached down and took her hand in his. It felt cold, but was as soft as ever. Her breathing was regular and smooth, and she seemed to be resting well.

"I love you," he whispered.

As John looked down at her, he began to feel very tired. The emotional ups and downs of this day were wearing on him. He knew he needed his rest, but he didn't want to leave her side.

"I'm sorry, but I have to take her vital signs."

John didn't respond other than to force a smile and move out of the way. He watched as the nurse did her job.

"How is she?"

"She's doing just fine. Why don't you go get some rest? It will be quite awhile before she wakes up. You don't want her to see you all tired out, do you? Besides she'll need your support in the morning when we get her up."

"I guess your right," John said reluctantly. "I'll be back early."

"When she wakes, I'll tell her you went to get some rest."

"Thank you," John said.

John leaned over and gave Mary another kiss on the forehead. He looked at her for a minute, then turned to leave. As he was leaving the recovery room, he saw a uniformed police officer standing just outside the door. He felt a little uncertain about it, yet at the same time he felt relieved.

As John walked into the waiting room, the first thing he noticed was another police officer standing next to the door. Bill and Julie were sitting on a sofa. They looked up when he came in.

"How is she doing?" Julie asked.

"She's resting well. Where are Kay and Tom?" John asked.

"I don't know. Kay said something about having to talk to someone. They left in kind of a hurry."

It had been a hard day and John was too tired to think about that now. He had enough on his mind without worrying about what Kay and Tom were doing. He could talk to them later.

"I think it's time for us to go home," John said.

"Excuse me, Mr. Blake. I'm Officer Graham. I've been assigned to stay with you until we find out what is going on. Lieutenant Palmer has instructed me to take you to a safe house for tonight."

"Do you really think that's necessary?" John asked.

"I think it's a good idea," Bill said. "At least until they have a better idea of who did this and why."

"Okay," John said reluctantly. He was too tired to argue the point. "You might as well go home. I'll go with Officer Graham."

"We'll see you tomorrow," Bill said.

Julie stood up and gave John a hug. Bill gave John a reassuring pat on the shoulder.

John looked at the officer. The officer turned and started out the door with John following. Bill and Julie followed them as far as the rear hospital entrance.

Officer Graham stopped John at the door. He motioned for John to wait while he stepped outside. After Officer Graham was satisfied that all was clear, he motioned for John to come out. Officer Graham stayed close to John as they walked out to the police car.

"Do you really think this is necessary?"

"I don't know, Mr. Blake, but I think it's better not to take any unnecessary chances."

Officer Graham kept looking around as he opened the car door. John got into the police car and watched Bill and Julie leave as he waited for Officer Graham to get into the car.

John rode in silence as the officer drove to the safe house. It was a bit of a relief to know Mary was going to have a police guard tonight, too. He was sure he would sleep better knowing she was safe.

CHAPTER EIGHT

THE SUN WAS SHINING through the dingy windows of Mike's apartment when he finally woke up. It took him a few minutes to figure out where he was. He sat up on the bed and swung his legs over the side. The sudden weight on his ankle as he tried to stand quickly reminded him of the fall he had taken last night on the back steps.

He limped over to the front window and looked down at the street below. A dark blue car with black wall tires and a spotlight was parked across the street. He immediately recognized it as an unmarked police car. As he watched the car, he tried to decide what he should do. His first thought was to get out of his apartment and go to his secret hiding place as quickly as he possible. It was so close, but with the police right outside it seemed so far away.

Mike backed away from the window and looked around the room. Some of his pills were still scattered on the floor. He began picking them up and putting them in a bottle. When he was finished, he gathered what he had in his apartment that he could use and might need and put them in a small backpack. He knew that he couldn't risk being seen for at least a few days, and coming back here would not be wise.

As soon as he was ready, he went to the window and looked out. At that very moment, another car pulled up to the curb. A man got out of the car and walked up to the police car. The officer seated in the car pointed toward Mike's window.

Mike jumped back away from the window and leaned against the wall. He could feel a dull pain begin in his head again as his mind tried to deal with the growing feeling of being trapped. He grabbed his backpack, opened the door and peered out into the hall. It was clear. He quickly moved toward the back stairs.

He limped out onto the landing, then immediately jumped back inside and leaned up against the wall. His heart was pounding in his chest and his head began to throb. Two policemen were coming up the alley. He could feel the panic build inside him as sweat formed on his forehead. He looked toward the front stairway, then toward the back door. He needed a place to hide. He couldn't return to his apartment, they would be there at any minute now. He knew that the old man who lived across the hall wouldn't hide him. They had never gotten along very well. His only hope was to hide in the utility closet and hope that no one searched it.

Mike heard the front door at the bottom of the stairs open, then close. He quickly moved into the utility closet, closing the door as quietly as possible behind him. He crouched down on the floor and held his breath as the sound of footsteps drew closer, then stopped.

LIEUTENANT PALMER KNOCKED on the door to Mike’s apartment, then glanced at Officer Wallace as they waited and listened. There was no answer. He knocked a second time, again no answer.

"This is the police, Mr. Flanders. We would like to have a word with you."

"Do you think he's in and just not answering?" Office Wallace asked.

"I don't know. I think we had better break it in."

Lieutenant Palmer looked at Officer Wallace as he reached under his sport coat and drew his gun. They quickly swung around at the sound of a door opening behind them.

An old man was standing in the doorway of the apartment. His eyes were as big as saucers when he found himself looking down the barrel of Lieutenant Palmer's pistol.

"Please don't break it in. I'll open it for you, sir," the man said as he showed Lieutenant Palmer the ring of keys.

"Who are you?"

"My name is Sam Holder. I take care of the building," he said looking up at Lieutenant Palmer for the first time.

"Do you know if Michael Flanders is in?"

"I don't believe he is, sir. I haven't seen him since yesterday."

Lieutenant Palmer reached out for the keys. The old man picked out the key to Mike's apartment and handed the key ring to the lieutenant. Lieutenant Palmer unlocked the door and swung it open. He entered carefully, guns at the ready while looking in all directions. No one was there. Officer Wallace followed Lieutenant Palmer into the apartment with the old man close behind.

"About what time did you last see Flanders?" Lieutenant Palmer asked while Officer Wallace began searching the apartment.

"It must have been about seven, or seven-thirty yesterday evening."

"Lieutenant, I think you should see this."

Lieutenant Palmer turned toward the officer to see what he had found. He was holding up a wet shirt that had blood stains on it.

"There's also wet pants, shoes and sox under the bed."

"That's the shirt Mr. Flanders was wearing last evening. I sleep pretty sound, he must of come back, then left again."

"Do you have any idea where he might have gone?"

"No, sir. He has some place he goes to on his days off, but I don't know where it is."

"Do you know where he works?"

"At the Amoco gas station at Prospect and Cross, I think. Mr. Flanders is not very sociable, he doesn't talk much."

"That will be all for now, Mr. Holder. If you see Flanders, don't tell him we've been here. Just give me a call at this number," Lieutenant Palmer said while handing Mr. Holder one of his cards.

Mr. Holder glanced at the card as he left the room. Lieutenant Palmer closed the door behind him.

There was very little furniture in the room. One large overstuffed chair, a single bed, a dresser and a breakfast table with two chairs. One corner of the room served as a kitchenette. The sink was full of dirty dishes.

As Lieutenant Palmer looked around the room, he stepped on something that crunched under his foot. He stepped back and looked down to see a white powder on the floor. He knelt down to examine it closer. In doing so, he noticed a pill bottle just under the edge of the bed. Reading the label he discovered that the medication had been issued through the state mental hospital's pharmacy. He couldn't pronounce the name of the medication and had no idea what it was used to treat.

"Wallace, take this bottle to the state hospital. I want to know what this stuff is, what it's used for, and why it was given to Flanders. And find out who his doctor is, and what he's being treated for," Lieutenant Palmer ordered. "And send Sergeant Bergen up here on your way out."

"Yes, sir," Officer Wallace replied taking the bottle.

Lieutenant Palmer continued to look around. He began by going through the dresser drawers. There were very few clothes in the dresser, but under some T-shirts he discovered a box of .22 caliber cartridges. They were the same brand as the ones in the rifle found at the scene of the shooting. However, they would be of little value because they were a very common brand that was sold at most discount and hardware stores in the area.

Continuing his search, he found a shoebox in the bottom drawer. Opening it he discovered several photographs of Mike. The most recent photographs were taken inside a building with Mike in military style clothing and holding a rifle. A quick look around the room made it obvious that the pictures had not been taken here.

One picture showed Mike holding a rifle very much like the one found after the shooting. It was impossible to be sure if it was the same one until the photo could be enlarged.

"You wanted to see me?" Sergeant Bergen said as he entered the room.

"Bergen, I want you to put a twenty-four hour a day stakeout on this apartment. Something tells me Flanders won't come back here, but we need to watch his place, just in case. I think we have a good suspect for last night's shooting," Lieutenant Palmer said as he held out the pictures.

While Sergeant Bergen looked at the pictures, Lieutenant Palmer decided to look inside an envelope he found in the bottom of the shoebox. He opened it and found six pictures of a young girl. The pictures were old and a little faded. One of them looked like it might have been a graduation picture like those exchanged by the kids when they graduated from high school. The others were pictures of the same girl apparently taken during some high school functions. Turning the graduation picture over, he found writing on the back. It was a name, 'Mary Weston'.

"Well, this sure ties him into our case," Lieutenant Palmer said to himself.

"What have you got?" Sergeant Bergen asked.

"Pictures of Mary Weston. Now what would someone like Flanders be doing with pictures of Miss Weston when she never liked him? It might make sense if he had pictures of some of the other kids from high school in this envelope, but all of these are pictures of only Miss Weston.

"I want Mike Flanders found and picked up."

Sergeant Bergen nodded and left the room. Lieutenant Palmer continued to look around the apartment. Once he was satisfied that there was nothing else of importance in the apartment, he left, locking the apartment door behind him. When he reached the bottom of the stairs, he stopped and looked back toward the apartment. He had a gut feeling that someone was there, someone he had not seen. He shook his head, then went back to his car. Sitting in his car, he took a few minutes to think. He didn't like the feel of this case at all.

MIKE HAD HEARD some of the conversations, but only bits and pieces of it. He had not heard enough to know just what he should do, but he seemed to comprehend that his apartment would not be safe any more.

When he heard Lieutenant Palmer leave, he let out a sigh of relief. He found he was able to relax a little, but continued to stay motionless in the closet. Gradually, his headache began to subside. As it did, he was once again able to think clearly.

Mike had to think of a way to get to his secret hiding place without being seen. He knew that he would be safe there. As he thought about how to get away, he remembered the skylight in his apartment. It might allow him to get onto the roof. He wasn't sure what good it would do him, but it was all he could think of at the moment.

As quietly as possible, he opened the closet door and looked out into the hall. The hallway was empty. Mike quickly went across the hall and into his apartment. Once inside, he moved along the wall and looked out from the corner of the window. The police car was still parked across the street.

He looked up at the skylight, then pulled his dresser to the center of the room directly under the skylight. It was then that he realized the police had been in his dresser. He immediately checked his shoebox and discovered that his pictures of Mary were gone.

The anger he felt over the missing pictures caused the pain to start up again. It started at the back of his head and swiftly moved up and over the top of his head. He quickly realized that if it continued, he could lose control and pass out before he got to his secret hiding place.

He swore to himself. He had to move fast. If he took any of his pills, he might not be able to climb down off the roof of the building without falling.

Mike carefully climbed up on top of his dresser and forced the latch open. He pushed the skylight open, then pulled himself out onto the roof and closed the skylight.

Crouching down, he crawled across the roof to the end of the building. After looking over the edge to make sure there was no one around, he swung his legs over the side and slid down onto the fire escape. When he reached the bottom of the fire escape, he dropped to the ground and scrambled into a doorway.

Mike pressed himself up against the door while he took a minute to catch his breath. His heart was beating rapidly, and his head was pounding like someone was hitting him with a mallet. His ankle was also throbbing something fierce.

Making sure the coast was clear, he worked his way along the building to the alley. Looking down the alley, he could see a policeman standing next to a patrol car, but he was looking the other way. Since Mike couldn't go that way, he would have to try to get across Cross Street and work his way around behind the buildings on the other side of the street.

He limped across the street trying to blend in with the other people. Once across the street, he ducked into another alley. He hid behind a dumpster in an effort to relax for a minute in the hope of relieving some of the pain in his head and in his ankle. His head was hurting so badly that he tried to relieve the pain by rubbing his temples, but it didn’t help much.

As soon as he was able, Mike walked behind the buildings toward River Street. It was tough going for him with his sprained ankle and pounding headache, but he finally made it to River Street. He crossed River Street and the railroad tracks, then worked his way behind the old Hudson Auto Dealership. After climbing a fence, he hid behind one of the old cars. He closed his eyes and tried not to think in an effort to get the pain in his head to diminish a little.

Now that the tension of getting away from the police had subsided a little, his head didn't seem to hurt as much. He reached into the pack, removed a bottle of pills and took two of them. It never occurred to him that he had become dependent on the pills in order to simply survive daily life.

Mike had to cross the street again, and this worried him. Getting across the street once was one thing, but getting away with it twice was a different matter. His thoughts were interrupted when he heard a train whistle in the distance. The train offered him a quick and easy solution. He would be able to cross the street directly into the alley behind the Thompson Building while the train was between him and the police.

Mike waited for the train. He could feel the pills starting to take effect. As soon as the train blocked the intersection, Mike walked across the street and entered the rear of the Thompson Building.

By the time he got to his secret hiding place in the Thompson building and he was safe inside, the pills were once again clouding his judgment. He was already planning another attempt to rid himself of John, but he was also trying to think of a way to get even with Mary for betraying him.

In his present state of mind, he now saw Mary as the fickle one. In his warped mind, she was now the one to blame for the police hunting for him, for him not shooting John, and even for his sprained ankle. She would have to be taught a lesson.

Mike laid down on his sofa to plan his next move. He was soon asleep from the drugs.

CHAPTER NINE

JOHN RETURNED TO THE hospital about eight-thirty in the morning with Officer Harris hot on his heels. He went directly to the reception desk.

"I'd like to know what room Mary Weston is in, please?" John asked.

The receptionist looked through the card file. She noticed the card had written on it that Mary was not to have visitors.

"I'm sorry, sir. She can't have any visitors," the receptionist stated flatly.

"What do you mean, 'no visitors'?" John asked, the tone of his voice showing his impatience with her.

"Just a minute," Officer Harris interrupted. "Is that the doctor's order, or by order of the police?"

"I don't know, sir," she replied nervously.

"Why don't you find out? Call the doctor. I would like to talk to him," Officer Harris directed her.

The receptionist picked up the phone, dialed a number, talked to someone, then hung up. She looked up at Officer Harris.

"Doctor Mathers will be with you in a minute."

John looked at Officer Harris and smiled as if to say 'thank you'. He hoped Mary's condition had not gotten worse overnight, and that the "no visitor" order was simply for her protection.

Within a couple of minutes, Doctor Mathers came to the receptionist desk. He smiled when he saw John. John felt a little relieved to see that the doctor was smiling.

"Good morning, John. I trust you got some rest?"

"Yes, I did. How is Mary?" John asked impatiently.

"She's just fine. She's a little tired and has a little discomfort from her injury, but she's doing well. She's looking forward to seeing you.

"Can I see her now?"

"Of course. I just left her. She will most likely doze off and on most of the day, but that's normal. She's in room 215."

"Thanks, Doc."

The doctor gave a slight nod acknowledging the thank you. John went directly to the elevator with Officer Harris following close behind. They rode the elevator to the second floor.

When the doors opened, John looked down the hall. He immediately saw a police officer outside a room. It gave him a secure feeling to know that Mary was being protected.

John walked toward the door. The officer at the door tensed, but relaxed when he saw Officer Harris nod that it was okay. John nodded to the officer at the door, then slowly pushed it open. He peered in to see if Mary was awake.

Mary was lying against some pillows with her eyes closed. John entered the room as quietly as possible. She opened her eyes and turned to see who had come into the room. As soon as she saw John, a big smile came over her face.

"How are you doing?" John asked, relieved to see her smile.

"I'm okay," she replied obviously glad to see him. "How are you?"

"I'm fine."

John went to her and took hold of her hand. He leaned down and kissed her. He let go of her hand long enough to pick up a chair, set the chair next to her bed and sat down.

"Not a very good way to end a date," John said as he tried his best to cheer her up.

"What happened? I know I was shot in the back, but why?"

"No one seems to know why."

"Why is there a policeman outside my door? Do they think someone will try to shoot me again?"

The worry in Mary's voice and the look on her face was all too obvious. She was frightened, and had every right to be.

"I don't know. Lieutenant Palmer will probably be talking to you today. He does have a suspect."

John didn't want to say too much, but he couldn't keep things from her, either.

"Who?" she asked as she looked into John's eyes.

"Lieutenant Palmer thinks it might have been Mike Flanders."

"What? Why would he shoot me?"

John hesitated a moment. He squeezed her hand gently, and looked down at it. Her hand appeared small in comparison to his. It felt soft and smooth, yet it had a certain strength to it.

"Tell me, John. Please," she pleaded.

"They don't think Flanders was trying to shoot you. They think he was trying to shoot me, but shot you by mistake when you stepped in front of me."

Mary looked at him. Now she was more confused than ever. Was Mike Flanders really involved in shooting her? Was he the one that had been frightening her? There were too many unanswered questions running around in her head.

"What's the matter? Do you hurt?" John asked seeing the confusion on her face and mistaking it for pain.

"No," she replied as she squeezed his hand and forced a smile. "I'm just tired."

"Why don't you rest a bit? I'll leave you alone for a little while."

She tightened her grip on his hand, and said, "Please stay. I don't want you to leave."

John didn't reply. He simply held her hand in his.

Mary closed her eyes. She did not sleep, but rather tried to decide if she should tell John about what had been happening to her these past few weeks. She opened her eyes and turned her head to look at him. She loved him so much.

"John, I have something to tell you that I think you should know, and maybe the police should know, too."

John looked a little puzzled, but said nothing. He just looked at her and waited for her to continue.

Mary told him about all that had happened to her since her return from Peru. She kept nothing from him.

John didn't say anything for a minute. His mind was trying to put it all into perspective. There was no question in his mind that Lieutenant Palmer would want to know about it.

Mary waited for John to say something, anything. His silence was disturbing to her.

"I better get hold of Lieutenant Palmer and tell him about this. It has helped me understand why you looked so tired when I first saw you last night. The whole thing just doesn't make sense, though."

"Nothing about Mike makes sense. I think he's crazy. I think he enjoys frightening me. I think he always has enjoyed it," Mary said.

"I agree. I'm going to see Lieutenant Palmer and tell him about this."

"Okay, but hurry back. Please," Mary begged.

John stood up, leaned over and gave Mary a kiss. Slipping her hand behind his head, she held him to her. Their kiss made her heart race and her breathing heavy. She moaned because of a little pain as her breathing became heavier. John straightened up and looked down at her. The worried look on his face told her that he was afraid he had hurt her.

"I guess I'm not quite ready for any heavy necking just yet," she said as she smiled up at him.

"You better get ready."

The note of humor in John's voice reassured her that he loved her and would stand by her.

"I'll be back soon."

John left the room. Officer Harris followed him to the elevator.

"I need to talk to Lieutenant Palmer right away."

"I'll contact him on the car radio."

"Good. Can we have him meet us someplace where we can get something to eat?"

"Sure."

JOHN FOLLOWED OFFICER HARRIS to his patrol car and made contact with Lieutenant Palmer. The lieutenant was on his way back into town from the state hospital and agreed to meet them at a coffee shop on Washington Street.

It took only about fifteen minutes for John and Officer Harris to get to the coffee shop. After getting coffee and a couple of rolls, they sat down at a table back in a corner to wait. John sipped his coffee and picked at the roll. He was not as hungry as he thought. His mind was trying to make sense out of all the confusion.

"You said it was urgent. What's up?" Lieutenant Palmer asked as he pulled up a chair and sat down across the table from John.

John filled Lieutenant Palmer in on what Mary had told him. Lieutenant Palmer listened, and seemed to understand.

"It doesn't make sense to me that he would frighten Mary when I'm his target. I think he was after her all the time," John said.

"I'm sorry, but I'm going to have to disagree with you. I think you will see my point after you hear what I found out this morning. In fact, it does make sense."

"What do you know that I don't?"

"I had a long talk with the doctor who treated Flanders in the state mental hospital. I also spent some time going over the county court records.

"According to Flanders' doctor, Flanders shouldn't have been released from the hospital. He was considered very unstable, but the board that holds hearings on each case before a patient is released, released him anyway. At the time, there was a strong movement to protect the rights of the mentally ill patient. The board felt his condition could be controlled by medication, and as far as they were concerned it was being controlled. What they didn't realize or didn't choose to understand was it was the medication that caused his personality to continually change."

"Why didn't they simply put him back in the hospital?"

"Good question, no good answer. It seems they didn't want to waste the time and money to look for him."

"They knew they had a dangerous situation on their hands, yet chose to do nothing about it," John said in disgust.

"There's nothing we can do about that now. Once we find Flanders, he will most likely go back to the state mental hospital. Right now, I want to tell you what we're dealing with, what kind of a character this Mike Flanders has turned out to be. He is a lot different from when you knew him in school," Lieutenant Palmer continued.

"It seems Flanders was arrested a number of years ago. He had used scare tactics to frighten a young woman. When she was so frightened that she couldn't even think straight, he kidnapped her and took her to an old barn outside of town.

"Now this is where it gets bizarre. He kept the woman a prisoner there for over two weeks. Every day he would go see her and feed her like a pet. In payment for the food, he would take a piece of her clothing. By the end of the week she had nothing left to wear. He did give her a blanket, which he would put over her when he left her. When he returned the next day, he would take it away from her.

"By the end of the second week, she was pretty much his to do with as he pleased. She was so frightened, hurt and humiliated, that she would do anything to keep him from hurting her any more."

"I've heard of that before. It's a form of brainwashing where humiliation is used to destroy a person's self-image, I believe," John commented.

"That's right," Lieutenant Palmer continued. "The young woman was very pretty when he took her. She was not so pretty when we finally got her back. It seems during the second week, Flanders would come to the building and untie her. By this time she was too scared to run. He would do all sorts of things to her.

"With all the trouble Flanders went through to get this woman to do anything he wanted, the records clearly state that he never had intercourse with her. He would touch her, fondle her and take pictures of her naked, but never had intercourse with her. He would even bathe her. He seemed to get his kicks from 'playing' with her and her mind.

"At his hearing, he was found to be mentally ill and committed to the state mental hospital. He was released about two, two and a half years ago. He was in the state mental hospital for only four years."

"Whatever became of the woman?" John asked.

"That's the irony of this whole damn thing. She's in a private mental hospital in northern Michigan. The criminal gets out of prison while the victim gets a life sentence. How's that for justice?" Lieutenant Palmer said with a note of frustration and anger in his voice.

"It's not fair," John said, not knowing what else to say.

"Well, I suppose you want to know what we're doing. It's really quite simple. We're looking for Mike Flanders. We think he's found some place to hold up, but we have no idea where. We don't think he has left town. There is no indication that he has any friends or family. We're talking to everyone we can find that might know him or where he might be. We're watching his apartment. This is one character we will keep looking for until we find him.

"Have you checked out the barn where he held the woman captive?" John asked. It was the first place that came to his mind.

"Yes. The barn was torn down shortly after Flanders was caught."

"I guess that's where I would have started looking."

"Does Flanders know where you're staying?"

"I don't think so. He could probably figure it out if he tried. Why?"

"We don't think it would be safe for Miss Weston to go back to where she was staying. If he can figure out where you're staying, then that's no good, either. We need a place where both of you could stay until we find him. It would make it easier for us if the two of you are in the same place," Lieutenant Palmer explained.

"I have an old family friend who has a cabin just outside of town along the river. Would that do?"

"It might work. Does Flanders know about the cabin or your friends?"

"I wouldn't think so. They were actually friends of my parents."

"It might work. When Miss Weston is released from the hospital, I want you to take her there. I don't want you to tell anyone, and I mean anyone, where you are until we can get a handle on this whole mess. Is that clear?"

"Yes. It should be no problem. I'll call and make arrangements for the use of the cabin. Now all I have to do is convince Mary, Miss Weston, to come live with me."

"Do you think that will be a problem?" Lieutenant Palmer asked, the look on his face showing some concern.

"I don't think so, Lieutenant," John said with a smile.

JOHN RETURNED TO THE HOSPITAL with Officer Harris and spent most of the day at Mary's bedside. He helped her get up and walk around to help her get her strength back.

John told her about the plans to stay at the cabin. Mary thought it would be romantic to sneak away to some little hideaway, just the two of them.

Over the next four days they talked, and Mary had time to regain most of her strength. The police had not been able to find Mike. It seemed that he had just dropped out of sight. An officer remained outside Mary's door twenty-four hours a day.

On Wednesday morning, Mary was discharged. John and Mary left through the basement garage in a service truck provided by the police department. They were driven to Ann Arbor where a car was waiting for them. From there, John and Mary drove to the secluded cabin.

A police officer was left outside Mary's hospital room for the remainder of the day, and her name was not removed from the list of patients at the reception desk until late that night. By the time anyone knew Mary had been discharged, she would have been gone most of the day.

IT WAS ABOUT NOON when John turned onto the narrow dirt lane that led down to the river. The trees were thick with their broad leaves forming a canopy over the road. The undergrowth was thick with its vines and beautiful wild flowers in full bloom.

As they drove into a clearing, the river was directly in front of them. Off to the side, tucked back in the trees, was a log cabin. John stopped the car, then watched Mary as she looked around.

"This is beautiful. You'd never guess we're only a few miles from the city. It's like an oasis, so quiet and peaceful."

The cabin was small, but well designed. The screened in front porch ran the full length of the cabin to allow for sitting on warm summer evenings, even when the mosquitoes were out.

"Ready to go in?"

John didn't wait for an answer. He got out of the car, walked around to her side and opened the door. He took her hand and led her to the cabin.

"Are you hungry?"

"A little real food would taste good after hospital food," she replied as she looked around the cabin.

"Go ahead and look around while I fix something. Would sandwiches be okay?" he asked.

"That would be fine. I'm not really all that hungry. I'm a little tired though."

"Maybe you would like to take a nap after lunch."

"I think I will," she said standing in the doorway and looking into the bedroom.

The bedroom looked very inviting with its queen-size bed. There were two dressers, a chair and a dressing mirror. A full bathroom, complete with tub and shower, was located off the bedroom. The cabin had all the conveniences of living in town with the seclusion of living in the country.

John watched Mary as she looked over the bedroom. He smiled as he thought about what might be going through her mind with only one bed.

"That's your room. I'll sleep on the sofa."

She turned around and looked at him for a moment, then walked up to him. Putting her arms around his neck, she looked up at him. He wrapped his arms around her waist as she leaned against him.

"Now that I have you trapped in this beautiful, romantic cabin, a million miles from civilization, do you really think I would let you get away from me that easily?"

"I sure hope not," he said smiling back at her and pulling her tightly against him.

She groaned slightly as he squeezed her.

"You're going to have to be a little careful how hard you squeeze me for a while. I'm still a little tender. Sometimes my muscles tense up and make my back ache."

"I'm sorry," he said as he loosened his hold on her. "I didn't mean to hurt you."

"I know you didn't," she said as she smiled up at him.

"Tell you what, let's have some lunch, then you can lie down. If you like, I'll give you a back rub guaranteed to relax every muscle in your beautiful body."

"Now that sounds great."

He leaned down and kissed her gently. She held onto him, savoring the gentleness of his kiss.

"Sit down and I'll get us something to eat."

John reluctantly let go of her and she sat down at the table. She watched him as he made sandwiches and poured milk. After setting their lunch on the table, he sat down across from her.

"What would you like for dinner tonight?" John asked.

"Are you doing the cooking?"

"Of course. I can't let my patient do it."

"How long will I be your patient?"

"A couple of days, then you can cook."

"Oh. In that case I best enjoy it while I can. What are my choices for dinner?"

"Just about anything you want. We have a full refrigerator and freezer. How about steak and salad, and maybe a little wine? If the wind is up enough to keep the mosquitoes away, but not blowing too hard, we might build a fire down by the river and roast marshmallows while we watch the sun go down. How's that sound?"

"That sounds wonderful."

She smiled at him. This was better than any dream she had of them together, she thought. She was feeling relaxed and comfortable for the first time in weeks.

After they finished their lunch, he walked her as far as the bedroom door. It was still hard for her to believe that she was here with him.

"You get ready for your nap. I'll come in after I finish cleaning up the kitchen to give you that back rub I promised."

John kissed her lightly on the lips, then guided her on into the bedroom.

Mary could hear him in the kitchen as she sat on the edge of the bed and took off her shoes and sox. She crossed her arms in front of her and pulled her sweater up over her head. She laid her sweater over the chair. Unhooking the side of her slacks, she slipped out of them and laid them on the chair with her sweater.

She took a minute to look over her shoulder at her reflection in the dressing mirror. There on her back was a three-inch square bandage covering the stitches. The area around the bandage was black and blue. She sighed softly.

Mary pulled the cover off the bed, folded it up and laid it on the foot of the bed. It was too warm for anything more than just a sheet. She crawled into bed and pulled the sheet over her. With her head comfortably cradled on a soft pillow, she closed her eyes and let her mind wonder while she waited for John.

A question she had asked herself at the Class Reunion came to mind. Had John changed any? It gave her pause to think, to think about the night at the Class Reunion when John had held her and kissed her with the same kind of gentleness that he had shown when they were in high school. She smiled to herself as she thought that nothing had really changed between them. They were simply older, and hopefully, wiser.

AFTER JOHN FINISHED THE DISHES, he walked through the door into the bedroom. He could see that Mary was not asleep. There was a soft pleasant smile on her lips. The years had done little to change her. She was a very good-looking woman. He walked up to the side of the bed and sat down beside her. She opened her eyes and looked up at him.

"How do you feel?" he asked. His obvious concern for her showed in his voice.

"I'm fine. I'm just a little tired."

Mary was not sure if she was feeling better because she was out of the hospital, or because she was away from all her worries, or because she was with John. But, it really didn't matter. The important thing was that she was here with him.

"Would you like me to go and leave you to rest?"

"Not just yet. I want you to kiss me and give me that back rub you promised me, the one guaranteed to relax every muscle in my body," she said as she smiled up at him.

"Well, it will be hard, but I think I can manage."

John smiled down at her as he leaned over her. She raised her arms and wrapped them around his neck. Their kiss was long and loving. It was a gentle kiss, yet had a touch of passion that made their hearts beat almost as one.

"Mmmmmm," she sighed as their lips parted. "I love you," she whispered as she looked into his eyes.

"I love you, too," he whispered. "I think maybe you best get some rest before I decide to climb under these sheets with you."

"I might not mind that," she replied playfully.

"Don't press your luck lady. I can only restrain myself for so long," he said teasing her.

Mary looked at him. She really did love him. She felt very much at ease with him.

"How about that back rub and some rest?" he suggested.

"I think I could use both."

"Roll over on your stomach."

Mary rolled over and John carefully pulled the sheet down to the small of her back. The sight of the dressing and the black and blue area on her back made him stop and take notice. It was the first time he had seen her injury. It was obviously healing very well, but the sight of it made him angry. His anger quickly subsided as he reached up to the center of her back and unhooked her bra. Except for the black and blue area around her wound, and the three-inch square bandage, her back was smooth.

John placed his hand at the base of her neck and gently began to knead her tight muscles. He worked the muscles of her shoulders, neck and across her shoulder blades. Gradually, her muscles began to relax and the stiffness and soreness began to subside.

"Mmmmmmm. That really feels good. That's so much better."

"I'm not done yet. Just relax and wander off into dreamland. Are you tender anywhere other than around the bandage?"

"No."

"Okay. Close your eyes and relax," he said.

Now it was time to help her get the rest she needed. Placing his hands flat on her back, he began to gently rub her back. John used very little pressure, but simply let his hands glide over her soft skin. Being careful not to touch any area that might be tender, he continued to gently slide his hands over her back from the base of her neck to the small of her back. It didn't take long before she succumbed to the gentle motion of his hands on her skin.

As soon as John was sure that Mary was sleeping, he eased himself off the bed. He stood there looking at her for a minute. Mary looked beautiful lying there, so much at peace.

"You have taken very good care of yourself," he said silently to himself.

John carefully pulled the sheet up over her back. He wanted to lie down beside her, but he decided against it. She needed to rest more than she needed him to keep her awake.

Leaving the bedroom, he went into the living room where he sat down in an easy chair. He put his feet up on the coffee table and leaned back. He had not realized how stressful these past few days had been on him until this moment. Within a few minutes, John was fast asleep, too.

CHAPTER TEN

JOHN WOKE WITH A START. Something was very wrong. He could hear Mary cry out. He jumped up and ran into the bedroom. He instantly realized that Mary was having a nightmare. He sat down on the edge of the bed and gently shook her to wake her. Her eyes flew open and she sat up. He took her in his arms and held her. He could feel her body trembling with fear.

"It's okay. It's okay," he said softly, trying to reassure her that she was safe.

Gradually, she realized where she was and began to understand that she had been dreaming. She wrapped her arms around John's neck and held onto him for dear life. As she began to regain her composure, she laid her head on his shoulder and cried softly.

"It's okay, you're safe with me," he assured her.

He held her in his arms and comforted her until she stopped crying. As soon as she had settled down, he gently pushed her back a little so he could look into her eyes. She looked up at him.

"You're all right. I've got you," he said softly.

Her dream had shaken her. Her outburst had also embarrassed her.

"I'm sorry," she said as she looked up at him.

"You're all right now. Why don't you go back to sleep? I'll be in the other room if you need me."

"Don't go, please. Stay with me," she pleaded.

She knew she would feel more secure with him beside her, and she needed him close.

"Okay. I'll stay, but you need to rest."

John smiled at her, but he was unable to hide his concern. He gently laid her back down on the bed. He noticed that her bra had fallen away from her breasts when she sat up, but she made no attempt to cover herself. He stood up and walked around to the other side of the bed. He placed a pillow up against the headboard of the bed, then sat down and swung his legs onto the bed.

Mary slipped her bra off her arms and laid it on the bedside table. She felt no embarrassment having him see her naked to the waist, it seemed as natural as loving him. She curled up on her side and placed her head on his lap with her arm across his legs.

John ran his fingers through her hair and gently rubbed her back and shoulders. She moaned softly as he gently touched her. She was once again able to let herself relax. It was not long and she was again feeling safe and secure, finally dozing off.

John looked down at her half-nude body. She was as pretty as ever, maybe even prettier, he thought. He reached down and pulled the sheet up over her, then tipped his head back against the headboard and fell asleep.

JOHN COULD HEAR THE squirrels scampering around in the trees outside the window. Mary was still curled up beside him with her head on his lap. He didn't want to wake her, but it was getting close to suppertime.

Mary moved slightly, curling up a little tighter against him. She moved her hand on his leg. He smiled down at her, knowing that she was waking up.

"Comfortable?" he asked softly.

"Yes."

"Did you sleep well?"

"Mmmmmmm. Very well."

"Feel like getting up?"

Mary felt secure right where she was. She rolled over and laid flat on her back. She tipped her head back to look up and saw him smiling down at her.

"Slide down here with me," she said as she patted the bed beside her.

John slid down along side her and slipped an arm under her head. She rolled up against him, resting her arm across his chest and her head on his shoulder. With the warmth of her breasts against his side, he gently slid one hand up and down her arm while he gently stroked her shoulder with the other.

Mary listened to the beating of John's heart. The thought ran through her mind that she felt as protected as a kitten lying next to its mother. She opened John's shirt and ran her hand over his chest. She liked touching him almost as much as she liked having him touch her.

They laid together for almost an hour, enjoying the comfort they gave each other. It was a quiet and peaceful time for them. It was a time that they needed to feel close, and to bathe in the warmth of their love for each other.

"I suppose we should get up," Mary said reluctantly.

"Whenever you want. We don't have to do anything you don't want to do. What do you say we take a walk along the river before dinner?" he suggested.

"It's been forever since I've done that."

The thought of it brought back memories of a time long ago when she had enjoyed being alone with him along this very river.

"I think the last time I enjoyed a walk along the river was with you. We went to the park near Delhi," John reminded her.

"Did you really enjoy it?" she asked.

"I enjoyed everything we did together, except when we broke up."

The thought of them breaking up hit a sad note for Mary. It was something she had not thought about for some time.

"Well then, maybe we should do it all again, except for the breaking up part," she suggested.

John squeezed her gently. He was afraid to squeeze her too hard. The last thing he wanted to do was to cause her pain.

Mary looked at him as he tipped his head toward her. Their lips met in a tender, yet passionate kiss. As they kissed, he gently rolled her over on top of him. The warmth of her breasts against his bare chest stirred his heart.

As their kiss ended, she rolled off him and onto her back. Mary watched him as he sat up and swung his legs off the bed. He started to leave the room, but stopped at the door. He turned around and looked at her. He couldn't help but notice the smooth lines of her body as she lay on the bed.

"Wear something comfortable to walk in. There's a little cafe down the river near the bridge. We'll go out for dinner tonight," John suggested.

"That sounds nice."

"It's only about a mile if we walk along the river. That won't be too far for you, will it?"

"No. The doctor told me that walking would be good for me."

"I thought since this is such a nice evening we'd walk down to the cafe to eat, instead of having steaks."

"We can have the steaks some other time," she said with a smile.

John returned her smile, then went into the other room leaving her to get dressed.

He hasn't really changed much, she thought. Mary remembered that he had always been concerned about her and her feelings. It made her feel good that he still cared. It seemed that it had been a long time since she had felt good about anything.

She lifted the sheet and sat up. It hurt her a little to sit up from a lying position, but she knew that would get better soon. As she stood up, she looked over at the mirror in the corner of the room. The reflection she saw was that of a woman in her mid-forties who really didn't look that old. She looked at her figure. Her breasts were still firm and round, her stomach still flat and smooth, her waist narrow, her hips well shaped, and her legs looked pretty good, too. She smiled at the reflection and was glad that she had taken care of herself.

Mary was also pleased that John had taken care of himself. Maybe, deep down in the back of their minds they had known that some day they would meet again and find the love that they had lost.

It passed through her mind that this was all a dream. Things seemed to be going very well between them. Almost too well, she thought as her own insecurities crept into her thoughts.

Mary turned and picked up her bra and went into the bathroom. When she came out, she dressed in the same clothes she had on earlier. She could change later when they get the luggage from the car. Besides, her light blue slacks and sweater showed off her shapely figure very nicely.

As she sat down on the bed to put on her shoes, her mind was consumed with thoughts of John and herself. Her heart kept telling her that she was doing the right thing by not holding back from him, but her head was still telling her to slow down. She wondered if John remembered why they had broken up in high school, she certainly did.

"I had a thought," John said as he stepped into the doorway to the bedroom interrupting her thoughts. "I don't think we should go to the cafe tonight. We're supposed to be in hiding until they find Flanders."

"I think Lieutenant Palmer would be upset if he found out we were going out to a public place for dinner," she agreed.

"I think 'upset' would be an understatement. Maybe we should have those steaks and a salad now, then go for a walk after dark. The moon should be full tonight," he said with a big grin.

"I'd like that. What can I do to help?" she asked as she stood up.

"Well, you can make the salad, if you feel up to it," John suggested.

As Mary walked passed John, he slipped his arm around her shoulders and she put her arm around his waist. After walking the few steps to the refrigerator, John stopped and took Mary in his arms. He leaned down and kissed her. She returned his kiss with only a sample of her love and desire for him.

"We will starve to death if we keep this up," she said as they broke off the kiss.

"Maybe, but what a way to go," he replied grinning at her.

Mary gave him a squeeze, then let go of him. She opened the refrigerator and handed him the plate with the steaks, then took out the makings for a dinner salad.

When dinner was ready, they sat down and ate. After dinner, they cleared the table. Mary washed the dishes while John dried them and put them away. It seemed so natural for them to be together, doing things together.

The thought passed through Mary's mind that right now was how it would be if they were husband and wife. She felt happy and content. Her head was still telling her to slow down, but her heart kept reminding her that she had lost him once before and not to lose him again.

John was feeling very content, too. He didn't want to push her into anything, but he could hardly keep himself contained. He thought about how he had let her get away from him, and that he would not make that mistake again.

JOHN WAS FOLDING the dishtowel and hanging it up to dry while Mary was wiping off the table. John watched her as she leaned over the table. She has a very good figure, he thought to himself just as she turned around and caught him looking at her.

"What are you looking at? As if I have to ask," she said smiling.

"You."

"I can see that. Do you like what you see?" she asked playfully.

"Well, it's not too bad, I guess," he replied kidding her.

"What do you mean 'not too bad'?" She stood flat-footed with her hands at her hips.

"Well, you could use a little more padding back there," he said as he leaned to one side and pointed toward her rear. He was able to keep from laughing, but he couldn't keep the silly grin off his face.

"Well!" she said trying to act irritated, but not doing very well at it.

She threw the wet dishrag at him, but John ducked. The dishrag hit the cabinet behind him and fell onto the counter. He advanced toward her, looking at her with as sadistic a grin as he could muster up without breaking into laughter.

Laughing, she turned and ran for the bedroom. Just inside the bedroom, she turned toward the bathroom. At the end of the bed, John caught her arm and turned her. Mary fell onto the bed with John falling beside her. He put his arms around her and rolled her over him.

She lay on top of him with her arms wrapped around his neck. The laughing soon died down as they looked into each other's eyes. Slowly, she leaned down until their lips met. Their kiss gradually became deeper and more passionate, and she moaned softly as he held her tightly over him. She smiled at him as she rose up on her elbows and looked down into his dark brown eyes.

"Do you really think I need more padding?"

John slid his hands over the smooth contours of her butt. He gently rubbed her, feeling the smoothness of her curves and the firmness of her shape.

"Not a bit. I like your butt just the way it is," he said a little short of breath.

She smiled at him and laid her head on his shoulder as he continued to rub her. It felt so good to have him touch her. She murmured softly enjoying his touch and the feel of his body under her.

"I love you," she whispered softly.

"I love you, too."

The spell was quickly broken when John forgot about her injury and ran his hands up her back. As his hand touched the area that was still very tender, she flinched from the sudden sharp pain.

"I'm sorry," he said as he quickly lifted his hands from her back. "I didn't mean to do that."

She rose up on her elbow and once again looked into his eyes. She could see that he was hurt almost as much as she was, maybe more.

"I know you didn't mean it," she said reassuringly. "Maybe we should go for that walk."

"Sounds like a good idea."

He gently rolled over allowing her to slide off him onto the bed. She rolled onto her back while he sat up on the edge of the bed. She reached over and touched his back. He looked over his shoulder at her and smiled.

"A penny for your thoughts," he said.

"I was just thinking how gentle you are with me. When I think back to when we were in high school, that is the one thing I've always remembered about you," she said thoughtfully.

"I think we should go for that walk before you embarrass the hell out of me," he said as he stood up and reached out to her.

Mary sat up on the bed and swung her feet onto the floor. She reached out and took his hand, letting him pull her to her feet. Letting go of her hand, he put his hands along the sides of her face. He tipped her head back a little as he leaned down and kissed her again.

Mary wrapped her arms around his waist, pulling herself up against him. She felt the warmth of his kiss go through her entire body. At this moment, she knew what it meant to be in love, really in love.

THE SUN WAS SETTING as Mary and John walked out of the cabin into the warm evening air. The color of the sky went from a light blue in the west to a deep purple in the east. The evening star was shining brightly and a gentle breeze blew in across the water leaving little ripples on the surface of the otherwise smooth river.

John and Mary walked hand in hand toward the beach. John stopped suddenly and signaled to Mary to be still. He pointed toward the beach where it sort of melted into the forest. Standing at the river's edge was a white tail buck that was looking at them. Behind the buck, they could see a doe drinking from the river. The doe seemed to feel safe and secure with her mate at her side.

John and Mary stood quietly, watching the deer. Mary slipped her arm around John as he put an arm around her shoulders and nestled her close to his side. Mary thought about how safe the doe must feel with her mate standing beside her. She glanced up at John. She had her man beside her, too.

"It seems we are not the only ones who think this is a lovely night for a walk," Mary said in a whisper.

John smiled at her, squeezed her lightly and said, "I guess not."

John and Mary walked off in the opposite direction the deer had taken. They walked along the path in silence.

John stopped, and Mary turned to face him. She reached up and wrapped her arms around his neck, drawing herself close to him. The moonlight reflected in her sparkling eyes.

"You are beautiful," he whispered.

"Kiss me," she replied with a slight smile.

John smiled, then lowered his head to her. Their lips met in a kiss that was gentle and soft. Gradually, the kiss became more passionate. Their lips parted and their tongues played together. John held her tightly against him.

The passion of their kiss almost consumed them to the point of not knowing, or caring, where they were at this moment. They were in each other's arms and that was enough.

Reluctantly, their kiss ended. Mary rested her head on John's shoulder. She was breathing in short, almost gasping breaths. Consumed by their passion, she had hardly noticed how much it hurt for her to breathe so deeply. She could hear John's heart beating as fast as hers.

Mary continued to lean on him until her breathing became more normal and the discomfort of deep breaths faded away. It was not easy for her to regain her composure with her body pressed against his and his hands placed firmly on her butt.

Even in the midst of their passionate, demanding kiss, he was still gentle with her. He placed one hand at the back of her head and gently rubbed the back of her neck. She murmured softly at his touch.

"Shall we start back?" he asked in a soft quiet tone.

"Maybe we should," she agreed, not really wanting to let go of him.

He took her hand in his and they walked back toward the cabin without saying a word. Each was deep in their own thoughts. When they arrived back at the beach, John wrapped her in his arms, careful not to touch her back where he might cause her pain.

"Wait here," he said softly as he looked at her face.

He let go of her and walked toward the cabin. She didn't know what he was doing, but she trusted him completely. Mary stood there on the sandy beach looking toward the cabin, waiting for him to return. Before long, he came back carrying a blanket.

John laid the blanket out on the sand, then took her in his arms and gently laid her down. Lying down beside her, he propped his head up on one hand and looked at her. Once again the moonlight shone on her face and made her eyes sparkle. As he looked at her, she put her hand behind his head and drew him toward her.

John leaned down to her until their lips met. As their kiss grew deeper and more passionate, she rolled up against him.

After their long passionate kiss, John rolled onto his back and gently tucked her up against his side with her head resting on his shoulder. He lay quietly looking up at the sky, but his mind was not on the stars. His mind was on the woman lying beside him. He wanted her, not just to make love to, although he did want that. He wanted to wake up next to her every day for the rest of his life. He knew that was what he wanted, but maybe it wasn't what she wanted.

"What are you thinking about?" Mary asked softly.

"Oh, I was just thinking about us," he replied.

"What about us?"

"Well, it's kind of hard to explain."

"Why don't you try?"

Mary needed to know what was on his mind, but was a little afraid it wouldn't be what she wanted to hear. The weeks before he showed up had been hard on her self-image. It was still difficult for her to believe anything good would last.

"We parted many years ago. Yet, when I saw you at the dance, it was as if we had been apart for only a few days. It was as if the years we were apart had never been. Do you know what I mean?"

"Yes, I think so," she said as a lump began to form in her throat and tears came to her eyes. Mary understood what he meant. She understood more than he could realize.

"Seeing you at the dance was like - - - like it had been when we were in high school. I felt kind of a - -, well - -, a happiness seeing you again. It was like a blankness - - - or an emptiness, - - or a loneliness, when you were not with me. But when you were there, I felt whole again," he said trying to pick his words carefully so she could understand, but still having a hard time finding just the right words to let her know how he felt.

"I guess I'm rambling now, but do you understand what I'm trying to say?"

Mary didn't answer him. She couldn't say anything because of the big lump in her throat, but she understood every word he had said. Tears were running down her cheeks. Why had they wasted so many years? Why had she been so stupid? She couldn't answer her own questions for there were no answers to the things that had happened so many years ago.

John realized that she had not answered his question, although he was sure she had heard him. He reached down and took her chin in his fingers and gently lifted her face so he could see her eyes. Her eyes had always told him what was going on in her head. As he looked down at her, he saw the moonlight sparkle off the tears on her face.

"I'm sorry. I didn't mean to make you cry. I'm sorry."

At that moment, he felt he had hurt her again some how.

"No, no," she cried softly as she squeezed him tightly. "It makes me sad to think of all the years we could have had together if I hadn't been so stupid when I was younger."

"What's that supposed to mean?"

John was confused. Trying to think back, he couldn't remember her ever doing anything that could possibly be considered stupid.

"Remember when we broke up after our junior year?" she asked.

"Yes. I remember, but I don't remember why we broke up."

He was now more confused then ever. He didn't know what that had to do with now.

"We broke up because I was told that you were making passes at Sondra Hamilton." Her voice quivered.

"Sondra Hamilton!"

"When I saw you outside the gym talking to her, I figured my friends had been telling me the truth."

"I never made a pass or anything like it at Sondra Hamilton. But if that was why we broke up, why didn't you confront me with it?" he asked.

"I couldn't. I was so hurt, yet I loved you so much."

"I still don't understand. I don't remember having any kind of fight or argument. I don't remember anything about it for that matter."

He was sure that he would have remembered if they had a fight, even a little one.

"I know it's silly, but at the time I couldn't confront you with what I believed to be true. I trusted you with my heart, and I loved you so much it hurt not to be with you. Just to be held by you, just to stand next to you, would have been enough. When summer came, I just let our relationship grow apart."

"So that's why I didn't hear from you while I was working at the state park that summer. I thought you found someone else."

John began to understand what had happened. By thinking she had found someone else, he had let her go without confronting her. All he had ever wanted was for her to be happy.

"I let you think I had found someone else. It made it easier for me. It wasn't until after we graduated that I found out it had all been a lie. By the time I found out, you were off somewhere in the Navy. I didn't know where you were or how to find you. I wasn't even sure if you would have wanted me to find you."

"Well that's all over now. I think we should forget that part of our lives and think about the future. You are very special to me," he said as he kissed her lightly on the forehead.

Mary laid her head back down on his shoulder and held on to him. She was getting a second chance, and she was not going to waste it. She was not going to lose him again.

They lay quietly together on the beach for an hour or so. They listened to the sounds of the breeze blowing through the trees, the soft sound of the ripples of water splashing against a small log at the water's edge, and the sound of an owl in a nearby tree. This was a time for them to be close and enjoy the peace of their love for each other.

AS IT GREW LATE, the temperature began to drop. Mary snuggled closer to John. He wrapped her in his arms as best he could. It was comfortable for a while, but she was still feeling the chill of the night air.

"Would you like to go inside?"

"Yes, I think I would," she replied.

John stood up and helped her to her feet. He shook the sand out of the blanket and wrapped it over her shoulders. She smiled up at him as he put his arm around her shoulders and led her to the cabin. As they stepped up on the porch, he stopped and looked at her.

"You know, we never got our luggage out of the car. How about fixing some coffee while I get our things?"

"Okay. I'm interested in seeing what Kay packed for me to wear," she said before going into the cabin.

When John returned to the cabin with their suitcases, Mary was in the kitchen. She watched him as he carried their luggage into the bedroom. When he returned, she held out a mug of coffee. He took the mug and followed her to the sofa where they sat down.

"How are you feeling?"

"I feel very happy right now," she replied with a smile. "How about you?"

"I'm happy, too, but that's not what I meant."

"I know."

The tone of her voice was apologetic for not taking his question more seriously.

"I really feel pretty good."

John felt much better, but he was still worried about her.

Mary leaned against him, and he tucked her under his arm. They sat quietly enjoying the closeness of one another. After a while, Mary yawned.

"Bored or tired?" John asked, smiling at her.

"I'm sorry, I guess I'm a little tired. Would you mind if I take a shower and get ready for bed?"

"Not at all, I was thinking the same thing. Would you mind if I share the bed with you."

Mary looked at him and smiled.

"If you don't share the bed with me, I will never speak to you again. Plus, I'll cry a lot."

It was kind of an off the wall comment, but deep down inside Mary knew how much John hated to see her cry. She wanted him to know how much she wanted him to sleep with her tonight.

"I wouldn't want to be the one to make you cry," he said as he leaned over and kissed her on the cheek.

She stood up and walked around behind the sofa. Standing behind him, she put her hands on his shoulders. He tipped his head back and looked up at her.

"I'll be back shortly," she said softly.

"I'll be waiting."

She leaned over and kissed him on the forehead.

After Mary had gone into the bedroom, John put his feet up on the coffee table and sipped his coffee. He felt relaxed and comfortable.

"You won't believe this," Mary said from the door of the bedroom. "Kay didn't pack me a nightgown."

"That's okay with me. Maybe she didn't think you'd need one."

"I'll bet it's okay with you," she said grinning at him.

"If you need a nightshirt, in my suitcase is a pair of pajamas. You can wear the top, if you want,"

Mary smiled and returned to the bedroom while John picked up a magazine and thumbed through it. When Mary came back into the living room, she walked around in front of him. She was wearing his pajama top. The sleeves where rolled up to her wrists. It was buttoned from between her breasts down to the last button. The bottom just covered her beautiful firm rear while showing off her shapely legs. She was also barefoot, making her look even sexier and more desirable.

"Well, what do you think?" she asked as she struck a rather sensuous pose.

"That pajama top looks better on you than it does on me."

John looked her up and down before inviting her to sit down beside him. She sat down and curled her shapely legs under herself. Putting down the magazine, he leaned over and kissed her lightly on the lips.

"I'll be right back," he said as he got up. "Wait here for me?"

"Yes," she replied smiling up at him.

John went into the bedroom. After shaving and showering, he put on the bottoms of his pajamas. Before returning to the living room, he turned down the covers on the bed.

Mary looked up as he came out of the bedroom. She smiled as she looked at him. There was some gray in his hair, but he was still a handsome man.

"Well, what do you think?" he asked holding his arms out for her to look him over.

"Very nice, and sexy, too."

John walked around the sofa and leaned down. She wrapped her arms around his neck as he picked her up in his arms. She was more than willing to let him carry her to bed. She could think of nothing that would please her more than to have him want her, even desire her.

He carried her into the bedroom and gently laid her down on the bed. He pulled the covers over her. She watched him as he moved around to the other side of the bed. He shut off the light as he passed by the switch. Pulling back the covers, he crawled in beside her.

Mary rolled up against him and he wrapped his arms around her. Resting her hand on his chest, she curled her leg over his.

Moonlight made its way through the trees and into the window casting a soft glow over the bed. John put a hand on her leg. Her leg felt soft, smooth and warm. Rubbing her leg, he let his hand drift up over her shapely hip. She slowly rolled over on her back as his hand moved up across her flat stomach and up to her breast.

He propped his head up on one hand as he looked into her eyes. He pulled his other hand out from under the pajama top, then slowly unbuttoned it. He pushed it open, exposing her firm breasts and flat stomach.

"You're beautiful," he said in almost a whisper.

Love me," she said softly as she rolled up against him, pressing her firm breasts against his bare chest.

THE RAYS OF SUNLIGHT shone in through the bedroom window. The birds were singing and the squirrels were scampering in the trees. It was a beautiful morning.

Mary was curled up against John. The warmth of his body felt good against her skin. She opened her eyes and watched her hand rise and fall on John's chest with each breath he took. This was a very special morning for Mary. She felt soft all over, and very much a woman. Since graduation from high school, and through the years of loneliness in the mountains of Peru, she had often thought of John and how things might have been. She had dreamed about making love with him. Now her dream had come true.

MARY DIDN'T WANT TO leave this quiet, comfortable place at John's side. She fought the idea of getting up as long as she could, but when nature calls, you must answer.

Mary rolled away from John and sat up on the edge of the bed. A smile came over her face when she saw their pajamas lying on the floor. She loved him so much she couldn't find the words to tell him.

Just as she was about to stand up, she felt a warm hand lightly touching her back. She turned and looked over her shoulder.

"Good morning."

"Good morning," he replied.

"Your hand feels warm. I like that."

She enjoyed his touch and remembered how gentle he had been last night.

"I'd like to stay here and let you keep doing that, but I have to make a little trip to the bathroom."

"Well, I wouldn't want to keep you from your 'little trip'."

John watched the covers fall away from her body as she stood up. Standing in front of him was a beautiful naked woman, yet the one thing that caught his attention was the black and blue area around the bandage on her back. The grin on his face quickly faded as a twinge of anger ran through him.

Mary bent over to pick up the pajama top. She swung it over her shoulders and slid her arms into the sleeves as she went into the bathroom.

John lay back on the bed with his hands behind his head. The sight of her injury brought him back to the real world. He wondered if Lieutenant Palmer had located Mike Flanders. If not, he wondered how long it would take the police to find him.

He didn't want thoughts of Flanders ruining his days with Mary. Days they could use to get to know each other again. Days to help make up for the years they had lost.

He was still deep in thought when Mary returned from the bathroom. She smiled at him while he lay there looking up at her.

"What are you thinking about?" she asked as she sat down on the edge of the bed.

"I was just wondering if Lieutenant Palmer has found Flanders."

"I don't want to talk about that," she said as the smile faded from her face. "Right now, I'd like to have some breakfast. I'm starving. Why don't you get out of bed while I fix us something to eat?"

"Do I have to get up?"

"If you want to eat."

"When you put it that way, okay."

He reached out and grabbed Mary's hand. Gently, but firmly he pulled her over him. She willingly lay across his chest and relished in his touch as he wrapped his arms around her.

"I think you are the most beautiful woman in the world."

She smiled as she looked into his eyes. She couldn't resist reaching out and putting her hand on the side of his face. It was almost like a dream. She never believed that she would ever see this man again, yet here he was.

"Are you ready to eat?"

"What?"

His comment startled her. She had gotten lost in her own thoughts.

"I asked if you were ready to eat? Are you all right?"

"Yes, I'm fine. I guess I was just thinking about something else," she said with a smile.

"Do you want to let me in on it?"

"No. Maybe later." she said teasingly.

John reached out and took her hand again. He put it up to his mouth and kissed it, then let go of her. She stood up and blew him a kiss as she went into the kitchen.

Mary was frying eggs when John came into the kitchen. He walked up behind her and wrapped his arms around her. She leaned back against him as he kissed her just below her ear.

"That sure smells good," he said looking over her shoulder.

He slid his hands up her body and gently cupped her breasts.

"Mmmmm, you smell good, too," he added.

"If you don't quit, I may decide to let these eggs burn."

She enjoyed the feel of his hands on her breasts.

He let go of her and patted her on the rear. He went to the cupboard and gathered things to set the table.

"What do you want to do today?" he asked.

"The only thing I need to do is go to the doctor's office and get my stitches taken out. Other than that, there is nothing special I want to do, except spend the day with you."

"Well, we'll have to think of something to do," John said.

They sat down and enjoyed their breakfast together. After breakfast, they got dressed and drove to Doctor Mathers's office.

CHAPTER ELEVEN

THE SUN WAS SHINING through the cracks and holes in the boarded up windows of the old Thompson Building. Mike had opened up the second floor of the building so he could keep an eye on what was going on near his apartment. From the bow window in the front on the second floor, he could see both directions on River Street, and down the alley that ran behind his apartment only a block and a half away.

The morning light shone in on Mike as he laid on the floor. He got up and went downstairs to the back room. After securing the door, he laid down on the old green sofa and stared up at the peeling paint on the ceiling. He had been hiding in the Thompson Building since the shooting of Mary. He knew that the police were still watching his apartment, but his mind was trying to figure out what had happened to Mary and John.

He sat up and looked across the room at the phone. If Mary was still in the hospital, John would be close by. Mike had tapped into the phone line of a business that had an office in the building. He carefully picked up the receiver and listened. The line was not busy so he dialed the hospital.

After finding out that Mary had been discharged, he quickly hung up the phone. The news surprised and confused him. If Mary was no longer in the hospital, he might never be able to find them.

Somehow, in his confused mind, he was able to conclude that they would be together, but where? Where would they stay? Would they leave the Ypsilanti area for some place else, possibly for Colorado? No, he thought not. Mary had too many things unfinished. Maybe, they would go to her place, but something told him that they wouldn't go there, either.

Mike's head was beginning to hurt again. All this stress, all this thinking was starting to get to him. He had to find them, but he realized that he could do very little without a car. There was little doubt that his car had been hauled away from the parking lot and impounded by the police by now. They would also have his guns, except for one that he kept in a small drawer in his secret place.

There was one person that he knew who would come to him if he called. He went to the phone, picked up the receiver and dialed the number.

"Hello?"

"This is Mike."

"Mike! Where are you?"

"I need your help."

There was not even a hint of concern in his voice.

"I don't know if I can help you, Mike. They said on the news that you shot a woman. Did you shoot that woman?"

"I need your car for a little while. I know I can clear this up, but I need a car."

Marsha thought for a minute. She loved Mike even though he had hardly given her reason. He hadn't really treated her badly. He just didn't seem to care about her. In fact, he didn't seem to care about anyone. The only time he had any interest in her was when he needed sex. Deep down, she knew he didn't love her, but it didn't stop her from loving him. The only time he was mean to her was when he had those terrible headaches and they seemed to come more often over the past couple of months.

"Well?" he said demandingly.

Mike was getting impatient. He was starting to feel the pain in the back of his neck move up and over his head.

"Okay. I'll be over in a few minutes."

"I'm not at my apartment. I'm at my storage place."

"Mike, you're not doing anything that could hurt anyone, are you? I don't want to have to come see you at that hospital again. I don't like it there."

"I won't be going back to any hospital. I just have to clear this up," he assured her.

"Okay. I'll be over soon."

Marsha was not really convinced that he was telling her the truth. But if she didn't help him, he might do something that would get him sent away again. She wouldn’t like that one bit.

Mike hung up the phone without so much as a thank you. He knew she would do anything he asked.

MARY AND JOHN WALKED into the Doctor Mathers's office a few minutes after ten. John waited as Mary checked in at the reception desk. When she returned to John, she took his hand.

"It will be a few minutes before I can see the doctor."

"Okay," he said as he led her to a couple of chairs in the corner of the waiting room.

"You don't have to wait with me if you don't want to."

"I'll wait with you. When we're done here, I'd like to pay Howard Van Scott a visit since we are here. He sounded like he had some kind of a business deal I could get involved in."

"You mean he might have a job for you?"

"More of an investment, at least that was the impression I got. We didn't have much time to talk about it."

"Well, I'm stuck here until the doctor can see me. Why don't you go see him? His office is just a couple of blocks down the street, on the corner. You could talk with him for a little while, then come back and get me."

"Are you sure you'll be okay?"

"Of course," she replied with a smile. "Nothing's going to happen here."

Reluctantly, John stood up. He leaned down and kissed Mary lightly on the lips. He turned and left the office. He had some reservations about leaving her alone, but what could happen to her in the doctor's office?

John walked to Howard Van Scott's office. After he introduced himself to the receptionist, she escorted him into Howard's office. Howard greeted him, then they sat down to talk.

MARY WAS READING A MAGAZINE when the nurse called her name. She put down the magazine and followed the nurse into a treatment room. The nurse told her to take off her blouse, and that the doctor would be with her in a minute. She took off her blouse, then laid down on her stomach on the treatment table. It seemed like a long wait before the doctor came in

"Hello, Mary," Dr. Mathers said as he entered the room.

"Hi."

"Well, let's see how you're doing."

Doctor Mathers sat down on a stool next to the treatment table and carefully removed the bandage over Mary's wound. With a great deal of care, he checked the wound.

"Well, it's looking pretty good. How does it feel?"

"It hardly hurts at all, only when I forget about it and bump it, or when John squeezes me too hard."

"John cares about you very much. Did he tell you that we all thought he was your husband?"

"No. He never mentioned it," she said flinching as Dr. Mathers touched a tender spot.

"Still a little tender right there? Well, that's to be expected. I think we can take these stitches out. It looks like it's healing nicely. The black and blue will disappear before long."

Dr. Mathers carefully removed the stitches, then cleaned the area again and placed a small bandage over the wound.

"There, I guess that will do it. You can put your blouse on and be on your way. You don't need to come in again unless you have a problem."

"How long do I need to keep it covered?" she asked as she buttoned her blouse.

"I don't see any reason why you can't take it off later this afternoon."

"Can I go swimming? We're staying at a cabin on the river."

"I don't see any reason why you can't. Just don't over do it. How is your breathing? Are you having any difficulty?"

"No, None at all."

"Good. You can do anything you feel like doing. Just don't put too much pressure on the wound for a few more days. It looks like it is healing just fine. I'd like it to continue."

"Thank you, doctor."

"You're welcome."

Mary returned to the waiting room and looked around, but John was not there. She glanced at her watch and realized she had not been in the doctor's office as long as she had thought. John must have figured she would be there much longer or he would have returned by now. She thought about walking over to Howard Van Scott's office, but hesitated.

It was only a couple of blocks to the office, so she decided that she would meet John there. She told the receptionist where she was going, then turned and left the doctor's office.

MARSHA PICKED MIKE UP at his secret hiding place. Marsha convinced Mike to let her drive. She knew how unpredictable he could be plus he was in no condition to drive. She followed his instructions, but it seemed that she was driving around with no clear destination. He didn't tell her what he was trying to do or where he wanted to go. She listened to him as he mumbled under his breath, but she could not understand hardly a word he was saying.

Mike paid little attention to Marsha as he looked out the window. He was trying to figure out how to find Mary and John, but the pain is his head would not allow him to think clearly or rationally. The pain was getting worse with each passing moment.

Suddenly, Mike saw Mary walking out of Doctor Mathers's office. It took a second or two for it to register in his clouded mind that she was there, actually right there in front of him. The hardest thing for him to grasp was that she was alone.

"There she is! Turn around!" Mike yelled at Marsha.

Mike's sudden outburst startled her. She wasn't sure who he was talking about.

"Who?" Marsha asked.

"Mary Weston. Turn the damn car around," he screamed angrily.

Marsha didn't know what she should do, but she knew better than to upset him any more than he was already. She had no choice but to do what he said, or face his wrath.

Mike couldn't believe it was going to be so easy. He knew the police were still looking for him. After all, they were still watching his apartment. It crossed his mind that it might be a trap, but how would they know he would be here? After all, he had stumbled on her by accident. He had no idea that she would be here.

Marsha turned into an alley, then backed out into the street to turn around.

"Get ahead of her and pull over. Leave the car running."

Marsha didn't understand what was going on, but she knew that if she didn't do what Mike demanded he would fly into a rage. There was no telling who might get hurt if he went into a rage. She pulled the car over to the curb, well ahead of Mary, and stopped.

"Get out and stop her," Mike yelled.

"What do I say to her?"

"I don't give a damn what you say, just get her to stop," Mike demanded.

Marsha could see that he was getting more agitated with each passing second. She thought about driving away, but she was afraid of him. She wanted to warn Mary, but she couldn't make herself do that, either.

Mike slumped down low in the seat as Marsha got out of the car. He waited until Mary walked passed. Reluctantly, Marsha stopped Mary at the front of the car.

"Excuse me, but are you Mary Weston?" she asked.

"Yes."

Mary immediately noticed that the woman seemed to be extremely nervous. She didn't know the woman and took a step back. Mary felt a cold chill run through her body and felt the need to get away as fast as possible. But before Mary could run, an arm came around her waist and a dirty hand clamped over her mouth. Mary tried to call out, but she couldn't make a sound.

"Get the door!" Mike yelled.

Marsha opened the back door of the car. Mike forced Mary into the back seat. Marsha just stood there watching with a shocked expression on her face.

"Get in the car," Mike demanded. "NOW!"

Marsha hesitated for only a second before running around to the driver's side of the car. As soon as the door slammed shut, Marsha shifted the car into drive and stepped on the gas. The car jumped to life. Before she realized it, she was speeding down the street.

"Slow down, damn it. You want everyone to see us?"

Mike was holding Mary and trying to keep her quiet. Mary tried to break free, but it was no use. He was too strong.

"Turn at the next corner and head for my storage place."

Mary was very frightened. She didn't understand what was happening, it had happened so fast. The more she struggled, the tighter he held her. Mary settled down when she realized that struggling was doing her no good. She would have to wait for an opportunity to break free.

Mike held his hand over Mary's mouth as Marsha drove the car to the Thompson Building. Once he convinced himself that he had gotten away, he relaxed his hold on her a little.

"You shouldn't have gone away with Blake. He has no right to you. You belong to me. Now I have a chance to get rid of him and have you, too."

Mary didn't know what was going on, but she couldn't allow her fears to take control of her, she had to think. She wanted to cry, but she fought back the tears as she began to realize that Mike thought he could get to John through her. It also began to become clear to her that Mike was as crazy as John had said.

When she turned to look at him, she could see a strange look in his eyes. His eyes were glassy and his pupils dilated. She knew he must be on some kind of drugs.

Once John found out she was missing, he would come for her. She knew that if Mike got another chance to kill John, he would. John had been right. Mike was out to kill him, not her. She couldn't let that happen, but what could she do about it?

Mary could smell the gasoline on Mike's hands, and the odor of his unwashed body. The smell of him made her want to vomit. Cold chills went through her and her skin was covered with goose bumps. It was hard for her to breathe with his dirty hand over her mouth.

"You don't need her, Mike. Let her go," Marsha pleaded.

"Just shut up and drive!" he yelled.

"I love you, Mike. She doesn't love you, she never has. I love you. You don't need her."

"I said shut up!" Mike screamed.

Marsha drove the rest of the way to the Thompson Building in silence. She pulled into the alley behind the building and stopped the car. Turning in the seat, she looked back at Mary. She could see the fear in Mary's eyes. She wanted to help her, but there was nothing she could do to control Mike.

"Get out and make sure there's no one around," Mike ordered.

Marsha hesitated as she looked from Mary to Mike.

"Do it." he ordered sharply.

She got out of the car and looked around. "I don't see anyone," she said as if she was disappointed.

"Open the door!"

Marsha did as she was told. She took the key Mike gave her and unlocked the door to the back of the building. After opening the door, she stood aside and watched as Mike dragged Mary from the car. Marsha was torn between her love for Mike, and what was the right thing to do. Should she stay with Mike, or try to run for help? She couldn't decide.

Mike shoved Mary through the door into the building. She stumbled over the threshold and fell hard on the dirty wooden floor. Mike grabbed Marsha's arm and jerked her into the building, then quickly shut and locked the door.

"Get over there on the couch."

Mary got up very slowly and moved across the room to the sofa, not once taking her eyes off him. Sitting down on the grimy green sofa, she huddled in the corner of it. She looked first at Mike, then at Marsha. Mary wondered what was going on in Mike's head? Did he really think he could get away with this?

Mary couldn't take her eyes off Mike for more than a couple of seconds at a time. He was crazy. If she said the wrong thing, or tried to talk to him, it could upset him even more. She sat silently on the sofa, watching, waiting. Waiting for what, she didn't know.

"Get me some rope out of that cabinet."

Marsha hesitated for a second, but only for a second. She opened the cabinet and saw all the books and magazines, and the pictures of nude women on the cabinet door. There was one other thing she saw in the cabinet, a box of ammunition. Although she hadn't wanted to believe that Mike had shot Mary, there was no doubt in her mind now.

She found the rope, then looked at Mary. Marsha was afraid for her. She didn't know how she could help Mary without putting Mike back in the state mental hospital, and that would mean losing him. She was confused. She knew Mike was crazy, but she still loved him.

"You stand over there," he ordered Marsha as he pointed toward the corner of the room.

"What do you think this will get you, me?" Mary asked defiantly.

"It will get me John. It's John I want now. I already have you."

Mary could hear the hatred in his voice and see it in his eyes. Mary's first thought was that no matter what, he would never have her.

Mike was beginning to pace the floor. Mary watched his every move. He seemed unable to concentrate, and had difficulty thinking. She also noticed that Marsha was still holding the rope, but Mike didn't seem to be paying any attention to her. Marsha was just standing in the corner like a frightened child watching him pace back and forth in front of the sofa.

Mike seemed to be showing signs of pain. Mary was not sure what the cause of the pain was, but it appeared to be the stress he was under. It seemed to her that the angrier he got, the more pain he had. Maybe it was the other way around, but it really didn't matter.

Mike suddenly stopped pacing, turned and looked at Marsha. He grabbed the rope out of her hands. He tied

Mary's hands and feet together. Mary could feel the anger in him as he tied her. The rope hurt her wrists and ankles.

Mike took a knife from the table and cut off the remaining rope. He motioned for Marsha to sit down at the other end of the couch. He then tied her hands and feet, too.

"What are you doing?" she asked, but she didn't resist.

"Shut up!" he yelled. His head was once again becoming so painful he was not sure how long he could stand it.

"Mike, please. You don't have to tie me. I wouldn't hurt you. I love you," Marsha pleaded.

Deep down in her mind, Marsha knew that Mike had gone past the point of returning to reality. She could no longer reason with him. She could no longer reach him.

"Shut up before I gag you."

Mike sat down in a nearby chair. The pain in his head was growing more severe with each passing moment. He put his head in his hands and tried to rub away the pain, but it didn't help. Nothing was going to help except for more pain pills. He was not so far out of it that he didn't know what would happened to him if he took them, but he also knew that he would pass out if he waited too long. He held off as long as he felt he could, but the pain continued to get worse.

Mike stood up and checked the ropes on Mary and Marsha. They both seemed to know that to say anything at all might cause Mike to explode into an uncontrollable rage.

He went to the sink for a glass of water. The pain was so great that it was difficult for him to see clearly. Without realizing it, Mike took four or five of his strongest pain pills, far more than the recommended dose and more than he was used to taking. He sat down in a chair to wait for the pain to go away.

Marsha noticed that Mike was not getting sleepy like he usually did when he took his pills. Instead, his eyes were becoming shiny like a cat's eyes when it's excited. A deep fear rose inside her as she realized that he had gone so far over the edge that it might be impossible to bring him back. She also knew he would become very excited and was capable of anything.

"Mary, don't do anything that will upset him. He can't control himself," Marsha whispered.

Mary looked at Marsha, then at Mike. She had never known such fear as she was feeling in the pit of her stomach at this moment. She was even afraid to move. Mary made no effort to make herself more comfortable as the ropes cut into her wrists and ankles. She could feel her heart beat in her chest, but it felt more like it was in her throat.

Mike jumped up. His sudden movement startled both of the women. He looked at Marsha, then at Mary. Without a word, he turned and started for the door.

"Where are you going?" Marsha asked.

Her voice was timid, yet demanded an answer. It was a spontaneous question, asked without any thought as to what might happen to her for asking. If she had thought about it, she would not have said anything.

He turned around and looked at Marsha, then at Mary. Ignoring the fact that Marsha had asked him a question, he walked up to Mary, reached out and took hold of her chin. He tipped her face up and looked into her eyes.

"I'm going to get John. I know where he is."

Mary couldn't keep her body from trembling. The look in his eyes scared her, but she couldn't let herself be the bait that would get John killed.

"And where might that be?" Mary asked trying to put as much defiance in her voice as she could muster.

"Where you were last, of course. At the doctor's office. You didn't think I could figure it out, did you?" he replied with a slight laugh.

Mary's heart sank. She knew John would return to the doctor's office for her. There was no way for her to warn him. At this moment, she felt more helpless than afraid.

Mike started to leave, but stopped and looked back at the women. He couldn't take the chance that someone might hear them if they called for help. He went to the cabinet for a rag and tore it into two long pieces. He put a gag over Marsha's mouth, then one over Mary's mouth. Once he was convinced that they couldn't scream or get loose, he turned and left.

Marsha looked at Mary. Mary could see the hurt in Marsha's eyes as they heard the door being locked from the outside. Marsha's eyes slowly filled with tears.

CHAPTER TWELVE

JOHN AND HOWARD talked longer than John had planned. John was feeling pretty good about the outcome of their first meeting. He hoped he hadn't kept Mary waiting too long. He walked briskly toward the doctor's office. He had some news he wanted to share with Mary and was sure she would be happy to hear.

When he walked into the doctor's office, he didn't see Mary. He concluded that she must be with the doctor. He felt a bit relieved that he hadn't made her wait for him. Picking up a magazine, he sat down and flipped through it.

The receptionist saw him come in, but didn't recognize him. After several minutes, she motioned for him to come up to the desk. At first, John didn't know if she was motioning to him or someone else. When he realized she was trying to get his attention, he walked across the room to the receptionist's desk. The receptionist held out a clipboard with a blank form on it.

"You have to check in before the doctor will see you."

"I'm not here to see the doctor. I'm waiting for Mary Weston."

"Miss Weston left about fifteen, maybe, twenty minutes ago."

He simply looked at the receptionist. He couldn't believe what he had just heard.

"She what? How could you just let - - sorry," he said as he stopped to gather his thoughts.

She was going to wait for him. Why had she changed her mind? Where would she go? The only answer he could think of was to Van Scott's office, but he had just come from there.

It was apparent that the receptionist was a little shaken by the way John had responded to her. If he was going to get any information out of her, he was going to have to keep his cool.

"When did she leave?"

"She left about fifteen, twenty minutes ago."

"Did she leave with anyone?"

"I don't think so. No."

"Damn! Did you see which way she went?"

"I'm sorry, I didn't notice."

"Did she say anything that might help me figure out where she was going?"

"She said she was going to walk somewhere to meet someone," she explained.

"Well, that would have been to meet me, but she never arrived. May I use your phone?"

She put the phone on the counter. He picked up the receiver and dialed. The phone rang only twice.

"Sergeant Bergen, can I help you?"

"Yes, this is John Blake. I need to talk to Lieutenant Palmer, right away."

"One moment, please."

John waited impatiently for the call to be transferred. It seemed to take forever. Finally, Lieutenant Palmer came on the line.

"This is Lieutenant Palmer."

"John Blake. Lieutenant, Mary's missing."

"What?"

"Miss Weston is missing."

"Where are you?"

John could hear the concern in the lieutenant's voice. He could sense that the lieutenant was upset with him, but it was too late to worry about that now.

"I'm at Dr. Mathers's office."

"I know where that is. I want you to stay there. I'll be there in a minute." Lieutenant Palmer hung up the phone without waiting for a response.

John looked at the receiver, then hung it up. He went outside where he waited impatiently, continually looking up and down the street. He knew there was no way Mary could have gotten lost. After all, she had lived in this town for years.

"Damn, I never should have left the doctor's office," he said to himself.

If Mary wouldn't walk off by herself, then she had to have been kidnapped when she left Doctor Mathers's office. He had no proof, but logic told him that Mike must have found her and grabbed her off the street.

John swung around as he heard the sound of a siren. A dark colored sedan with a small flashing red light on the roof pulled up to the curb and stopped with the squeal of tires. Lieutenant Palmer jumped out and ran around the car to John.

"Fill me in on what happened," Lieutenant Palmer demanded.

John explained why they had come to the Doctor's office. He then went on to what he believed must have happened. Two other police officers arrived and listened in. Lieutenant Palmer listened very carefully and formed a plan to find Mary as quickly as possible.

"I agree. She must have been taken right off the street. It had to have been Flanders, at least he is our best suspect," Lieutenant Palmer said.

"Mary would never have gone with him on her own. She was afraid of him. Someone must have seen him take her," John surmised.

Lieutenant Palmer nodded in agreement, then turned to the other officers. "I want one of you on each side of the street. Go door to door. Stop everyone on the street and see if you can find anyone who may have seen anything unusual.

A speeding car, an unusual sound, like someone trying to call for help, someone who appeared to be forced into a car, anything at all that might help us find Miss Weston."

"What can I do?" John asked as the officers began their search.

"You stay with me. We're going to walk back to the office where you were last. Mary must have been picked up somewhere in these few blocks. Someone must have seen something."

As they retraced John's path back to Van Scott's office, John watched the officers come out of one building after another with no sign of finding anything.

After all the shops along the street had been checked out, Lieutenant Palmer and John walked back to the police car with the other two officers. John stood next to Lieutenant Palmer's police car and listened as Lieutenant Palmer gave instructions to the officers to check all apartments facing the street above the stores for anyone who might have seen anything. John was deep in thought and didn't really notice the red sedan that was going by at a very slow speed. He just happened to glance up in time to see Mike Flanders behind the wheel.

"There's Flanders!"

In his excitement, he almost screamed at the lieutenant as he pointed at the red sedan.

Lieutenant Palmer turned to look. The red sedan suddenly sped off. Lieutenant Palmer ran around to the driver's side and jumped into his car as John jumped in on the curbside.

The other two officers ran to their cars as Lieutenant Palmer pulled away from the curb. With lights flashing and sirens wailing, they took off after Flanders.

"Did you get a license number?" Lieutenant Palmer asked as he wheeled around a street corner.

"I think so," he said then gave Palmer the license number.

John could hear the officers in the car behind them giving information to the dispatcher over the radio on their pursuit. As soon as there was a break in the report, Lieutenant Palmer quickly gave the dispatcher the license number of the red sedan, then dropped the mike on the seat.

John hung on as the car went speeding down the streets and skidding around corners. He knew Lieutenant Palmer was too busy driving to talk, and he was too busy holding on to say anything.

The red sedan made a sharp turn down a side street. It was over a block ahead of them. When they turned the corner, the red sedan was gone. Lieutenant Palmer pulled up to the next corner and looked both ways. They saw nothing.

"Damn!" he said as he hit his fists against the steering wheel.

He pulled his car over to the curb and let the other police cars continue to search for Flanders. John listened to the police radio as one of the officers from another car gave details of where they had lost Flanders.

John looked over at Lieutenant Palmer. It was clear that he was upset about losing Flanders. After all, he knew what kind of a man Flanders was.

As soon as the radio was clear of other chatter, Lieutenant Palmer picked up the mike and called the dispatcher. He asked for a new all points bulletin to be put out on Mike Flanders with a description and license number of the car he was now driving.

Lieutenant Palmer knew the car Flanders was driving was not his. The police had already impounded Mike's car. They had picked it up in the parking lot behind the Hoyt Meeting Center the day after the shooting. A check with motor vehicle records when they towed his car away had shown that there were no other cars registered to Flanders.

LIEUTENANT PALMER AND JOHN just sat there waiting for the information. Lieutenant Palmer wondered who owned the car Flanders was driving, and if it had been reported stolen. He had requested the name and address of the owner of the red sedan.

Finally the radio crackled and a voice said, "The car belongs to a Marsha E. Nicholson," and gave him the address."

Lieutenant Palmer shifted the car into drive and pulled away from the curb. He drove to the address he had been given, and parked out in front. It was a small modest house that seemed to have been kept in good repair. There was no car in the driveway. The garage door was open, but it was empty.

"Stay here," he ordered John.

Lieutenant Palmer got out of the car and walked to the door. He tried to look in the window next to the door, but couldn't see anything. He rang the doorbell and waited, but there was no answer. He tried the door, but it was locked. He walked around to the back of the house, looking in each window as he went by them.

"Can I help you?" The voice came from the house next door.

Lieutenant Palmer turned to see a woman watching him. He pulled his ID and badge out of his coat pocket and walked over to the woman. She looked at the ID very closely.

"I'm Lieutenant Palmer. I'm looking for Ms. Nicholson. Do you know if she is home, or where she might be found?"

The tone of his voice and the manner in which he asked his questions, seemed to put the woman at ease.

"No. I saw her leave earlier this morning. She left in kind of a hurry. I know she saw me, but she didn't say 'hello' like she usually does. She also left her garage door open. She always closes her garage door when she leaves."

"Do you have any idea where she might have gone?"

"No. I'm sorry."

"Does she have a husband, or maybe a boyfriend?"

"She doesn't have a husband, I'm sure about that. I think she has a boyfriend though. He's kind of a strange one."

"What do you mean by that?"

His interest heightened by the woman's use of the word 'strange'. This whole case was strange, and he knew Flanders to be strange.

"Well, I don't really know, he just seems to be, well, different, kind of strange, you know. I'm not sure, but he just reminds me of one of Miss Nicholson's patients."

"Patients? What does Miss Nicholson do?"

"Oh, I don't know what she does now, but she worked at the state mental hospital for a little while, and not too long ago. I believe she was a ward helper of some kind. She's not a nurse."

"Do you know where she works now?"

"No. I'm sorry."

"What does this boyfriend of hers look like?" Lieutenant Palmer asked.

"Oh, he's in his mid-to-late forties, a little older than Miss Nicholson. He must be under six-foot tall, dark brown hair with a little gray on the sides and dark wondering eyes. He always is looking around, won't look right at you.

"He has a little bit of a pot on him, maybe 240 to 250 pounds. Oh, I think he might be a mechanic. The few times I've seen him, he had grease or oil under his fingernails. You know, kind of dirty fingernails. I noticed that because my husband works in a garage. I know how hard it is for him to get that stuff out from under his fingernails."

"Thank you for your help."

Lieutenant Palmer nodded and returned to his car. John was standing next to the car waiting for him.

"Did you find out anything?" John asked.

John could see Lieutenant Palmer had a lot on his mind and simply waited for him to sort it all out. Once he did that, then, hopefully, John would get an answer.

The woman's description of Miss Nicholson’s boyfriend fit Mike Flanders to a T, but now he had another problem. Was Mike holding two women captive, or was one of them helping him? Where was he holding Mary? There appeared to have been no one else in the car. Was Miss Nicholson keeping watch on Mary while Flanders was out? If he had the two women, what was he doing out running around? Was he looking for John when he was spotted? All these questions and many more came to Lieutenant Palmer's mind, but none of them were getting answered. He could only speculate and that did him little good at the moment.

"What the hell's going on here?" Lieutenant Palmer asked himself out loud, more to hear his own thoughts than to get a response.

"What did you say?" John asked.

"Oh, nothing. It's just that this case has got me baffled. Nothing seems to make any sense."

"Maybe that's the problem."

"What? What do you mean?"

"Well, maybe nothing makes any sense because we aren't dealing with someone who makes any sense. We're dealing with a man who doesn't really live in our world. He lives in a world of his own making. I'm not sure he ever did live in this world," John said.

Lieutenant Palmer thought about what John had just said. Mike had been in the state mental hospital. He had done things most of his life that were not what would be considered normal, at least by normal people. Maybe, John had a point.

"That makes some sense, I guess."

Lieutenant Palmer motioned for John to get in the car. As John got in, the lieutenant got in behind the wheel. They sat there for a minute, both just thinking. They were trying to figure out where Flanders was hiding, and what he really wanted.

CHAPTER THIRTEEN

MARY COULD SEE the steady stream of tears running down Marsha's face. She understood, after all she was scared, too. Mike was out of control, and he was out looking for John. Even as frightened as Mary was, she was more afraid for John. She had seen the hatred in Mike's eyes. The thought that she might lose John again, only this time forever, was eating at her. She had to mentally shake herself so she could think about how she could help John. If she couldn't help John, the least she could do was to help herself. If Mike came back in the same condition he left, there was little hope of getting out alive.

It frustrated Mary that she couldn't move but a fraction of an inch at a time. As she squirmed to get free, she lost her balance and rolled off the sofa. She landed hard on the floor causing a sharp pain to run through her entire body. She cried out, but the gag muffled her cry of pain. Tears filled her eyes. She was afraid that she would pass out.

"Not now. Oh, please, not now" she pleaded silently.

Marsha saw Mary fall, but could do nothing to help her. In fact, she made no effort to even help herself.

Mary lay quietly on the floor waiting for the pain to stop. She wondered if her fall had broken open the wound, but she couldn't worry about that now.

As soon as the pain had subsided, Mary opened her eyes. There in front of her face was a small nail sticking out of the corner of the sofa. Inch by painful inch she squirmed closer to the nail. She hooked the rag on the nail and managed to pull the rag away from her mouth. She gasped in a breath of fresh air, at least the first breath of air that didn't smell like gasoline. Mary rolled away from the sofa and looked up at Marsha.

"Are you all right?"

Marsha nodded to indicate that she was all right, but her eyes didn't seem to agree. She made no effort to move.

Mary tried to sit up, but it was no use. Maybe there was something on the floor that she could use to get herself free, but she couldn't see anything.

"Can you see something sharp anywhere? Can you see anything, a glass, knife, anything?" Mary asked.

Marsha simply sat there looking down at the floor. She made no effort to look around the room. It was clear that she had already resigned herself to her end coming here in this dingy old building at Mike's hand.

Her unwillingness to help infuriated and angered Mary.

"Damn it, will you at least look? If we don't find a way to get loose and get out of here, there's no telling what he'll do to us before he kills us. You know he'll kill us, don't you?"

Marsha looked at Mary. It was clear from the look in her eyes that she knew Mary was right. She knew Mike was capable of killing them. It began to soak into her brain that her love for Mike wouldn't save her because he didn't love her.

"Help me, damn you!" Mary yelled.

Marsha was startled by Mary's outburst. She looked around the room. There was nothing on the coffee table, nothing on the end table and nothing on the counter, at least that she could see from the sofa. Marsha looked across the room at the small table next to the cabinet. There, under some papers, she thought she could see some kind of a knife, possibly a hunting knife. It was the knife that Mike had used to cut the rope.

Marsha looked at Mary, then back at the table, then at Mary, then back at the table again. Marsha's eyes widen with excitement. She tried to say something, but with the gag it was impossible for her to do anything but mumble.

"What do you see? Is there something over there?

Mary was almost too excited to realize Marsha couldn't answer her. Marsha nodded her head rapidly. Mary couldn't tell for sure what Marsha saw or where it was. She would have to ask questions Marsha could answer with a nod or a shake of her head.

"In the cabinet?"

Marsha shook her head.

"On the table?"

Marsha responded with a nod of her head.

Mary began inching her way toward the table. It was a slow and painful process. The ropes were cutting her more and more each time she tried to move, and the floor was dirty and rough.

Mary finally reached the table. Rolling back and forth against the leg of the table, she was able to jiggle the knife closer and closer to the edge of the table. Finally, with one last bump against the table, the knife fell off the edge of the table, almost striking Mary.

Mary squirmed around and picked up the knife. It was difficult, as her hands were growing numb from the lack of circulation. Once she had the knife in her hands, she began to slowly cut through the rope. Only able to move the knife a little at a time, and not being able to put much pressure on the blade, it seemed to take forever to cut throw the rope.

Suddenly, the knife cut through the rope freeing Mary's hands. Mary pulled the rope off her wrists and rubbed them to regain her circulation. The tingling sensations gradually went away and she was able to move her fingers freely. She picked up the knife and cut her legs free. She had to rub her ankles to wake up her feet. When she first stood up, she almost stumbled as the circulation in her feet was not fully restored.

"We've got to get out of here before Mike comes back," Mary said as she removed Marsha's gag and cut her loose.

"There is no way out except through the door we came in. Mike fixed it so no one could get in. When he did that, he fixed it so we can't get out, either."

Marsha's defeated attitude made Mary more determined than ever to escape. She looked at the door that led to the front of the building.

"Well, I don't intend to give up so easily. I'm going to find a way out of here. Where does that door lead?"

"It goes out to the front of the building. It used to be an office. I think he nailed it shut," Marsha explained.

Mary checked the door. It was nailed shut. She started looking for something that could be used to pry it open. There was nothing strong enough to use as a pry bar. The knife's blade wouldn't be strong enough.

One side of the steel cabinet was opened. Mary started to go through the locker, but it produced nothing but magazines and books. She found a couple of boxes of cartridges, but no guns. If they couldn't find a way out, maybe he left a gun in the cabinet. Someone would certainly come at the sound of gunshots.

Mary opened the other side of the cabinet. She noticed the sheet covering the inside of the cabinet door and jerked it off. She stopped suddenly. Her mouth fell open, and her eyes stared at what she saw. The door was covered with pictures of her. Seeing all those pictures sent a cold chill through her.

"Did you know about these?" Mary asked as she turned toward Marsha.

Marsha looked at the cabinet door. She had never seen the pictures before. Mike would never let her see what was in the cabinet.

"No," she said as she stared at the pictures. "That's you, isn't it?"

"Yes. Some of these pictures date back to junior high school. Some of them are pictures stolen from John's car when we were going together in high school."

It upset Mary to see that Mike had stolen pictures of her and John, and cut John out of the picture. It also angered her to see pictures that had apparently been taken of her without her knowledge. Why did he have so many pictures of her? There must have been three dozen of them. Mary was trying to figure out just what was going through Mike's mind to have saved all these pictures of her, none of them less then twenty years old.

"I helped take care of Mike at the state hospital," Marsha said. "He talked about you all the time. It was as if you were his one and only true love. He never mentioned you by name, but he said he had a lot of pictures of you.

"He never said any more about you after he was discharged from the hospital. He has been obsessed with you since seventh or eighth grade."

Marsha's voice carried the tone of a person who had found out about another love, one she could not compete against.

"I still don't understand. I never gave him any reason to feel the way he does. As far back as I can remember, he has frightened me," Mary said as if to apologize to Marsha.

Even though Mary couldn't understand why Mike "loved" her, she began to comprehend why Mike wanted John out of the way. She understood what had been explained to her, but she never really believed someone would react the way Mike had. She believed it now.

"We still have to get out of here."

Mary had let the pictures cloud her thinking for a moment. She quickly realized they were wasting valuable time, time they needed to find a way to escape.

"I don't think you're as safe with Mike as you think you are," Mary told Marsha.

"I'm sure you're right. I had hoped that he would grow to love me, but I think he's gone too far to turn back now."

There was a note of sorrow in Marsha's voice. She had loved Mike, but it had been a one-sided love.

They started toward the door to see if they could find a way to get it opened. Just as Mary reached for the door, she heard a key slip into the lock on the other side. Mary's heart raced, and her breath caught. It was too late. They had wasted too much time.

Marsha and Mary backed away from the door. Mary's mind was searching for a solution. Although she was frightened of what Mike might do to her, she couldn't give into him. She was not going to give up as easily as Marsha. For John's sake, she would fight him every inch of the way.

Mary looked around for something, anything. She saw the hunting knife on the floor where she had left it. She ran over to it and grabbed the knife off the floor just as the door opened. She swung around to face Mike with the knife in her hand. Raising the knife up, she held it out in front of her pointing the end of it at Mike. She had never been as frightened as she was right now, but he wouldn't have her, not without a fight.

As Mike entered, he seemed surprised they had gotten loose, but showed no sign of being upset over it. He simply smiled at Mary as if it were a joke, then glanced at Marsha. It was clear that Marsha was so afraid of him that he did not consider her a threat.

He looked back at Mary. It was easy for Mike to see how frightened she was. She was shaking so badly that she couldn't hold the knife steady, but he had no fear of her. He had taken so many pain pills that even if she cut him, he probably wouldn't feel it.

"Well, I see you got loose. You plan to use that or just stand there?"

"I'll use it if I have to," Mary said, her voice unable to hide her fear.

It was her fear of him mixed with the fear that she might never see John again that gave her the courage to stand up to him.

Mike just grinned and moved slowly toward her. She backed away from him, yet he closed the distance between them.

"Please don't make me use this," Mary pleaded.

As he continued to move closer to her, she grew more nervous. The closer he got, the more Mary was convinced she was going to have to use the knife on him. She could feel her heart pounding in her chest, and her breathing was coming in short shallow breaths.

"I don't think you have the nerve to use that on me," he said as he stepped closer.

"Don't Mike, please," Marsha pleaded.

"You stay out of this."

The tone in his voice was that of a man who would stop at nothing to prevent her from interfering.

Mike grinned at Mary, then quickly reached out to take the knife away from her. She stepped back quickly to get out of his reach and backed into the coffee table. She lost her balance, but swung the knife wildly to keep him back. As Mike grabbed for the knife, the sharp blade cut through the sleeve of his shirt and left a deep gash in his forearm.

Mary fell back over the coffee table causing it to collapse. She went crashing to the floor causing a sharp pain in her back and knocking the wind out of her.

Mike looked down at the blood running down his arm, but he felt no pain. He simply put his hand over the wound to stop the bleeding. While holding the wound, his eyes moved from his wounded arm to Mary lying on the floor.

Marsha could see the fury in Mike's eyes. The only other time she had seen him go into a rage was in the state mental hospital. She knew there was no limit to what he might do in such a state. She was convinced that he could kill without giving it a second thought. She knew she had to do something before he killed Mary. She hesitated for a second, then moved toward him.

"Mike, let me look at your arm. We have to stop the bleeding."

She spoke to him as calmly as she could. If she didn't speak to him in soft tones, he might explode and kill both of them right now.

As she drew near to Mike, he let go of his arm and swung his arm back. He caught Marsha on the side of her head. The blow sent her reeling back against the wall, where she fell to the floor.

It took a minute or two for her to recover. Marsha sat up and leaned back against the wall, afraid to get up. Touching the side of her face, she looked up at him. He had never hit her before.

"You stay out of this," he ordered.

The tone in his voice sent a shiver of fear through Marsha. Mary was right. Her love for Mike wouldn't save her from him.

Mike looked down at his arm. The blood was still running down it. He looked at Mary still lying on the floor. He was sure she was out cold.

"Get up and get the first aid kit out of the cabinet," he ordered as he looked toward Marsha.

Marsha didn't hesitate. Too afraid not to do as he told her, she got up and found the first aid kit.

Mike sat down at the table where he could keep an eye on Mary, then put his injured arm on the table. As Marsha went by Mary, she looked down at her. She wanted to help her, but was afraid to even try.

"Don't worry about her. I'll fix her when she gets up," Mike said.

Marsha sat down at the table and cleaned the wound. The cut was going to need stitches.

"You should see a doctor. The cut is really deep."

"I'm not going to any doctor. Just bandage it up and stop the bleeding," he ordered.

In silence, she placed a sterile pad over the wound, then wrapped it tightly with tape to stop the bleeding. As soon as she was finished, Mike pulled his arm away and stood up. He walked over and looked down at Mary.

"What are you going to do?"

"I'm going to get even for this," he said as he raised his bandaged arm up in a threatening manner.

Mary could hear him, but she did not open her eyes. The longer he thought she was out cold, the more time she had to think.

CHAPTER FOURTEEN

SUDDENLY A VOICE came over the radio.

"Lieutenant Palmer?"

"This is Lieutenant Palmer."

"Lieutenant, we have a lead on that car. Sergeant Bergen has spotted it in an alley off Cross Street."

"Where on Cross Street?"

"He said it's parked behind the old Thompson Building."

"Tell him not to go near it. He's to sit tight 'til I get there, and stay out of sight."

"Sergeant Bergen is parked around behind the old Hudson Dealership building. He suggests you approach from the south."

"Got it," Lieutenant Palmer replied as he pulled away from the curb.

John feared for Mary's life. He would have to keep his wits about him, or he would be no help to her. If he could keep a clear head, there was a chance everything would turn out okay.

They drove north on River Street across the railroad tracks and turned in behind the Hudson Dealership in the Historic District of Depot Town. Lieutenant Palmer parked behind another patrol car. Sergeant Bergen and another officer were squatted down behind some old automobile hoods, watching the rear of the Thompson Building. Sergeant Bergen moved away from his hiding place and walked back to meet them.

"Mr. Blake, Lieutenant."

"Fill me in, Sergeant."

"We think Flanders is in the Thompson Building. We found the car about a hundred feet down the alley next to a door. The front of the building is boarded up. We can't tell if he has holes to see out, or not. The front door appears to be locked from the outside with a large padlock. It may also be locked from the inside.

"The second floor has four windows off the alley, and four in front. We are checking around to see if anyone in the area has seen Flanders go in or out of the building," Sergeant Bergen explained.

"How are we set up?"

"We have two men across the street at the railroad depot. There are two cars over on Maple, at the other end of the alley. We also have a man in an unmarked car up the hill on Cross Street, in case he leaves. We have a man on the roof of the Hudson building. And we have the men you can see here with us."

"Good work, Sergeant. As best we can figure, Flanders is in there with Miss Weston and possibly one other woman. We think its Marsha Nicholson. We don't know what the relationship between Miss Nicholson and Flanders is, but she might be his girlfriend. She may be in this with him, or she may be a victim, too.

“There’s also the possibility that Flanders stole her car and she isn't even in the building. We just don't know."

Lieutenant Palmer moved along the side of the building and looked around the corner. He scanned the area in front of the Thompson Building for any signs of movement, then moved back and leaned up against the building to think.

It was clear that if anything went wrong, the officers at the railroad depot were too far away to be of much help. He wished there was some way to get someone closer to the front of the building. He wanted to know if Flanders could see out the front, and if there was some way of getting in the front.

While he was thinking about what to do, he looked back toward the other officer. He hadn’t noticed a man in a dirty old coat and hat standing next to a tree watching them. While looking at the man, an idea came to him.

"You. Come over here."

The man looked around, and then looked back at Lieutenant Palmer. He pointed at himself wondering if the lieutenant was talking to him.

"Yes. You."

The man looked at all the officers and decided it would not be wise to try to run. He walked cautiously toward Lieutenant Palmer. He had never seen so many police officers at one time, or in one place. He was thinking that he should have left instead of hanging around to see what was going on. Now that he had been called by the lieutenant, he was sure that he should have left.

"How would you like to sell your hat and coat?" Lieutenant Palmer asked.

The man looked at his coat, and then at the lieutenant. The look on his face showed he couldn't understand why a man as well dressed as the lieutenant would want to buy his hat and coat.

"How would you like to rent us your hat and coat for, say, an hour?" John asked. "I'll give you twenty dollars for the use of them," John offered.

John had a pretty good idea what Lieutenant Palmer had in mind. No one would think twice about a bum walking around the building.

"Well, I guess so," the man said reluctantly. "I get it back?"

"Sure, and the money. I'll even throw in a free meal," John added.

"You got a deal, mister."

The man took off his coat and hat and handed them to John. John passed them to Lieutenant Palmer, then gave the man two twenty dollar bills. The man looked at the bills as if he hadn't seen that much money in a very long time, which was certainly a possibility.

"You wait over there," Lieutenant Palmer told the man.

The man walked over to the tree and sat down. He watched as the lieutenant gave the hat and coat to Sergeant Bergen.

"Put this on, Sergeant. I want you to work your way along the front of the Thompson Building. Pick up a few things along the way. We want anyone who sees you to think you're just another bum picking through garbage. Don't spend too much time in front of the building, but look it over well. Keep your eyes open. Find out all you can, but don't do anything to cause suspicion."

"How about if I go around back, up the alley?"

"Good idea, but don't spend too much time around there. We don't want Flanders to get edgy."

AS SOON AS SERGEANT BERGEN was ready, he walked toward the Thompson Building. He had the hat pulled down over his eyes and the coat was baggy enough to cover his uniform and gun. He knew his dark blue pants and shiny black shoes would give him away, so he stayed close to the building. This way only the upper part of him would be visible from inside the building. If someone came out of the building, he could duck into a doorway. No one would think twice about it as it was a common practice of the homeless.

Sergeant Bergen moved from door to door. He listened and looked around, trying not to draw any attention to himself. After checking out the front of the building, he moved around to the alley. He moved closer and closer to the car, stopping to pick up an aluminum can here and one there.

Sergeant Bergen moved along side the car and looked inside. The keys were in the ignition and the window was rolled down. After taking a quick look around, he reached inside the car and grabbed the keys before moving on. Now that he was close to the building, he looked it over as quickly as possible. The door didn't appear to be locked from the outside.

When he got close to the door, he could hear voices inside but couldn't tell what was being said. It was impossible for him to look through the window. It had been painted over.

Sergeant Bergen moved on down the alley. When he came to a trash can, he stopped and began to rummage through it. As he looked back, he checked out the house on the other side of the alley. When he glanced up at the second story window, he saw a man duck back out of sight.

Sergeant Bergen continued down the alley to the end, making stops along the way at all the trash cans. When he reached the end of the alley, he ducked around the corner to a police car and called Lieutenant Palmer on the radio.

"Lieutenant Palmer."

"Palmer here. What did you see?"

"I'll fill you in when I get around there, but right now, there's someone in the house directly across from the car.

"I thought that house was empty."

"So did I, but there's someone in there, on the second floor."

"We need to get in there and find him. Maybe, he saw who went in the Thompson Building."

"I'll come around through the back yards and see if I can get into the house without being seen."

“Be careful.”

Lieutenant Palmer waited. There was nothing else they could do for the moment. It seemed to take forever before Sergeant Bergen voice came over the radio.

"We got him," a voice on the hand held two-way radio said.

"Let's hope he can be of some help." Lieutenant Palmer said as he looked toward John.

"Find out what he knows about who's in the Thompson Building," Lieutenant Palmer instructed the officer.

Lieutenant Palmer and John waited. John was growing more and more worried about Mary with each passing minute. He was sure that the longer they took to get her back, the greater the risk of her being hurt or even killed.

WITHIN A FEW MINUTES they saw a police car coming down River Street. The car turned in and stopped. Sergeant Bergen and another man got out of the car.

"Lieutenant Palmer, this is Mr. Thomas Wolff.

"Mr. Wolff, did you see anything strange or unusual going on at the Thompson Building today?"

"Yeah. It seems that this Flanders fellah comes over to the Thompson Building quite often, so I didn't think much of it when I saw him come out of the building this morning."

"Are you sure it was Flanders?"

"Yeah. I've seen him before. I've even talked to him, but he never says much. The sergeant here described this Flanders fellah you are looking for, that's him."

"Good. Go ahead. What did you see?"

"Well, I've never seen him there with anyone else before, but today he was there with two women."

“Tell me everything that happened that you can remember.”

“Well, earlier, I saw a woman drive up to the door. That would have been about, oh, maybe ten o’clock. Flanders came out and got in the car and they drove away. The woman driving and he was with her. I didn't see anyone else.

"After awhile, about an hour, maybe less, they come back. Only this time there's another woman with them. The woman who was driving the car earlier got out. Then Flanders gets out of the backseat. He had another woman with him. He had his arm around her and a hand over her mouth. It looked like he was kind of forcing her, you know, dragging her out of the car and into the building. Well, he didn't really drag her into the building. It was more like he pushed her through the door, and kind of hard, too.

"The first woman didn't like it, but she looked like she was going along with it. I can't really say, but she looked like she might have been afraid of this Flanders fellah, too" he explained.

"Did you see anyone else?" Lieutenant Palmer asked.

"No. No one else. I did see him leave in the car by himself, but he returned after a little while."

"Thank you for your help. If you don't mind my asking, why didn't you report this to the police?"

"Was none of my business," he replied, shrugging his shoulders.

"Thanks," Lieutenant Palmer said sarcastically as he shook his head in disgust.

Lieutenant Palmer looked over at John. They were both thinking the same thing. This was probably where Flanders had been all the time the police had been looking for him.

"Are there any other ways in or out of that building, like through the roof, or maybe the basement?" Lieutenant Palmer asked the Sergeant.

"No," the bum replied.

Everyone turned and looked at him. He had just been waiting around like he had been told, but he had been listening, too.

"How do you know that?" John asked.

"I know my way around all these buildings. There's no other way in or out of that building."

"Are you sure?" Lieutenant Palmer asked.

"Well, no, not for sure. I guess. Most of us stay away from that building."

"Why's that?" John asked.

"The guy that lives there, has guns and all kinds of things like that in there. One time, one of my friends got in the building. It was cold and windy. He was just looking for a place to get out of the cold and wind. He wasn't even in the part the guy uses. We found him the next day all bloody and beaten. When he came around, he warned us to stay away or that guy would kill us.

"You said you were told he had guns. Did your friend see any guns?" Lieutenant Palmer asked.

"All he said was the guy has guns in there. We didn't need to know more than that. He's a real nut. He's crazy," the man said looking at John.

John looked at the man's face and eyes. He was convinced the man was telling the truth.

"Thanks," John said.

"I think we have enough information to be sure they're in there. Call up the Swat Team," Lieutenant Palmer directed Sergeant Bergen.

"As soon as they get here and we've briefed them, we're going in. We can't wait any longer," Lieutenant Palmer told John.

"Wait a minute, Sergeant. Lieutenant, Flanders wants me. Maybe, I can get him to release Mary, and the other woman, in exchange for me."

John was thinking of Mary, a prisoner of Flanders. He didn't want her in there with him any longer than was necessary, and he didn't want her hurt because the police stormed the building.

"I don't think that will work. He wants you, but he wants you out of the way. I think he wants Mary, too. If you give yourself up to him, he will have both of you. Not a good idea," Lieutenant Palmer said shaking his head.

"I have an idea. It's going to be hard to get him out of there once he knows we're here, right?" John asked the lieutenant.

"Right." the lieutenant agreed.

"The longer we're here trying to figure out what the hell we're going to do, the greater the chance of him finding out we're here, right?"

"Right again."

"If I can get Flanders to come outside, or at least into the doorway, a sharpshooter in the second story window of the house across the alley could take him out with one shot, if necessary, of course.

"Flanders is mentally deranged and doesn't live in the real world so there's no telling what he'll do. I don't see as we have a choice. Anything else places too much of a risk to those inside," John explained to Lieutenant Palmer and Sergeant Bergen as calmly as possible.

"He just might be right," Sergeant Bergen said to Lieutenant Palmer. "The more people we have involved in this, the greater the chances of a civilian getting hurt. We have a lot of houses in the area. We don't have time to get everyone out. If we try, there's a chance we'll be discovered."

"I agree. Maybe, one of the officers could pretend to be you and get him to the door. No, that's no good. It wouldn't work. Besides it's too risky," the lieutenant said thinking out loud again.

"If I go, he would have to open the door. You said it yourself, he wants me. I used to be pretty good with a gun," John continued in his effort to convince Lieutenant Palmer.

"You give me a gun. If he won't come out far enough for the sharpshooter, I would be close enough to him to prevent him from hurting anyone else."

"Damn! I don't like it," Lieutenant Palmer said feeling frustrated.

The lieutenant knew that John's plan was the best plan they had going for them. He also knew that the longer they waited, the worse the situation could become. He also knew that once things went sour, they usually went sour very fast. With one, maybe two hostages, there was little chance of busting in and getting them out. The chances of loosing the hostages were very high, especially with someone like Flanders.

"What other options do we have?" Sargeant Bergen asked. "If we fill the alley with the Swat Team, the odds that someone will get hurt goes way up. If the Swat Team busts in, there's a likely chance of one of the women getting hurt, maybe both."

"I know you're right, but it's against the rules to use a civilian," Lieutenant Palmer said, his voice showing his frustration over the situation.

"Lieutenant, the rules can go to hell. I'm not waiting for your so-called "help" to come. If Flanders finds out the police are all over the place, do you think he's going to check a damn rulebook? Hell, no! He'll try to shoot his way out, and someone's going to get hurt or killed. I don't want it to be Mary. So give me a gun, or I'll go without one," John demanded as he held his hand out waiting for someone to put a gun in it.

The lieutenant stood there looking down at John's empty hand. He wanted to give John a gun, but knew if anything went wrong, he would lose his badge. But was his badge worth a human life? He reached under his sport coat and pulled out a 9mm automatic. He looked at the gun, then at John. Reluctantly, he placed the gun in John's hand.

"If it makes you feel any better, you can tell them I took it from you," John said as his fingers closed around the grip.

"Wait a minute. Sergeant, I want you in that window. Get a rifle and get up there. As soon as you're ready, let us know," Lieutenant Palmer ordered.

Sergeant Bergen nodded his head, went to his patrol car and drove away.

AS SOON AS SERGEANT BERGEN was in position to cover the alley door from the second story window of the house, he called on the radio to tell the lieutenant he was ready.

John moved to the front of the old Hudson building, then quickly ran across the street to the corner of the

Thompson building. Taking a deep breath, he peered around the corner. Looking down the alley, he planned each and every step he would take to get to the door.

“It's time”, he said to himself.

John moved along the wall, staying as close to the back of the Thompson Building as possible. He couldn't remember a time in his life when he'd been so nervous.

As John worked his way to the door, a quick glance up at the second story window of the house helped reassure him that he was not alone. He couldn't see Sergeant Bergen in the shadows, but he could see the end of his rifle sticking out of the window a couple of inches.

John stood with his back up against the building next to the door. He looked down at the 9mm automatic in his hand. It was time, and he was in position. The gun was ready, Sergeant Bergen was ready, and John was as ready as he would ever be. He listened carefully for any sound from inside the building, but heard nothing. He looked up at the window again for reassurance. He could still see just the end of the rifle barrel.

Sergeant Bergen leaned out into the light so John could see him. He nodded at John to indicate he was ready any time John was. John racked a cartridge in the chamber, then tucked the automatic in his belt behind his back.

Keeping his back against the wall, he reached out and knocked on the door. He waited for a response, but heard nothing. He knocked again.

CHAPTER FIFTEEN

THE KNOCK ON THE DOOR startled Mike. He never thought that anyone would find him in his secret hiding place. His mind was working fast in an effort to figure out what to do. His eyes quickly looked from the back door to the door leading to the front of the building. The drugs he had taken prevented him from thinking clearly. However, he did seem to understand that he might have trapped himself in his own hiding place.

John knocked again. Again there was no answer.

Mike looked around the room, then ran over to a small wooden cabinet. He took a small caliber pistol from inside a draw.

Mary took in a deep breath when she saw the gun. It hadn't occurred to her to look anywhere else for weapons. After all, she hadn't had much time to think about such things.

Mike moved toward the door, then stopped. He wasn't sure what he should do. He was growing more and more confused with each passing minute.

Marsha stood silently watching him. She was afraid of what might happen if Mike thought he was trapped. He had the look of a frightened and cornered animal.

"Mike. I know you're in there."

Mike recognized John's voice immediately. He looked at Mary who remained motionless on the floor, then at Marsha. Marsha was much closer to him. He grabbed her and pulled her close to him. Holding her in front of him, he pushed her toward the door.

"You alone?" Mike called out.

"Yes. I'm alone."

"Back away from the door so I can see you through the window."

John looked up at the rifle barrel sticking out of the second story window and motioned for Sergeant Bergen to pull back. Instantly the rifle barrel disappeared. John noticed a nail that was sticking out of a crack between the bricks. He quickly hung the pistol on the nail, then stepped back away from the building. He held his hands out so Mike could see that he was not carrying a gun.

Mike moved to the window and ordered Marsha to open it enough so he could see out. He looked out over her shoulder. He first looked at John, then at the house. He also looked up and down the alley, although he couldn't see very far either way.

"Keep your hands up and turn around."

John did as he was told. As he turned around, John saw several police officers moving into position. There were two officers at each end of the alley, close to the building. John understood Lieutenant Palmer's position in this, but hoped he would keep the men back.

"Stay right where you are. I have to think."

Mike was confused by the sudden turn of events. He was having difficulty thinking. This had not been expected. He had John right out in front of him, and this was the perfect opportunity to rid himself of him. Yet, his mind was trying to tell him that he was trapped. The confusion within Mike's mind was creating the kind of stress that caused him severe pain. His head was beginning to throb.

"What's the matter?" John asked, knowing Mike was in a state of confusion.

"Nothing. I have to think," Mike yelled.

"Come on. Get with it. You know you don't have much time. If I found you, the police will certainly find you. You know they will be here soon. You don't have time to think."

The rapid firing of statements by John confused Mike even more. His head was hurting more and more as he tried to think. With the confusion and stress John was building in Mike's head, even the medication Mike had taken was unable to control the increasing pain.

"Mike, you better make a decision. When the police get here, it will be too late. You'll go back to the state mental hospital. Only this time you'll never see the outside world again.

"If you've hurt Mary, I'll see to it that you live out the rest of your life in the deepest, darkest cell I can find in the state mental hospital. And you know I can do it."

John was trying to keep Mike's attention while hoping for the opportunity to get Mary away from him. He had no real plan, but hoped that Mike would open the door. John didn't really understand Mike very well, but he had seen people like him. He had to try to keep him off balance and stall while the police moved in closer.

"Listen, Mike. I'll make you a deal."

John started talking in a much calmer, softer tone. By talking very calmly after yelling at Mike, John hoped to keep Mike confused and a little off balance.

"You let me in, and let Mary go, and I'll see to it you're not hurt. How about it?"

"You're just trying to trick me."

"No. I'm not. You give yourself up and I'll see to it you get help to rid yourself of those headaches."

Mike was in such pain that he could hardly see, let alone make a clear decision. He wanted to get rid of the pain in his head, that much he could understand. He was beginning to feel as if his head was going to split wide open.

John's offer of help slowly sank deep into the recesses of Mike's mind and it began to register. He needed help. He understood that, even though the pain blocked out most rational thoughts. The pain was going to kill him if he didn't find a way to get it under control. He wanted help, but his mind kept telling him there was no help. The confusion between knowing what he needed, and the feeling of being trapped, was making the pain worse.

John was losing patience. He was worried that he might be pushing Mike too hard. There was no telling what Mike might do if pushed over the edge. His only thoughts were of Mary and her safety.

"Mike, I can get you the help you need. You know I can."

John was taking the chance that Mike could still think clearly enough to see that John was his only hope for any kind of help.

"Have I ever lied to you? You know I'll do what I say."

"Move up to the door. Don't try anything. I have Mary in here."

The quickness of Mike's response made John a little hesitant. Yet, at the same time, Mike's sudden change gave John a ray of hope. John knew it might be a trap, but that was a chance he would have to take. He would have to act quickly himself. He could hear the pain and confusion Mike was experiencing in his voice.

JOHN MOVED IN FRONT of the door. As he heard the door being unlocked, he quickly grabbed the gun from the nail and slipped it into his belt behind his back. When the door opened, he held both hands out so Mike could see that he didn't have anything in them.

John stood still, waiting to see if Mike would step closer to the door. Instead, Mike stood back and motioned for John to enter. John cautiously stepped through the door. Mike was still using Marsha as a shield. The pistol in his hand was pointed at John.

John quickly glanced around the room for Mary. He saw her lying on the floor in front of the sofa. His first thought was to go to her, to help her, but he thought better of it. With the way Mike felt about Mary, going to her aid as he had done in the past, might be all it would take to send Mike into a rage.

John had no idea what Mike would do in a rage, but he was sure that what little control he had of the situation would be lost. He also knew if Mike started shooting, every one of them might be killed. John wanted Mary as far out of the way as possible.

"Shut the door and lock it," Mike demanded.

John backed up to the door and pushed it closed. Without turning around, John reached back and slid the dead bolt into place, securing the door.

John once again looked at Mary. She seemed to be all right. She started to get up, but John made a slight motion with his head that told her to stay there. The floor was the safest place for her.

"What do we do now?" John asked.

The tone of his voice was quiet and calm, showing no sign of fear. He was afraid that if he showed any fear, Mike would take it as a sign of weakness. That would quickly reinforce Mike's confidence in himself, the one thing John didn't want to do.

Mike looked from John, to Mary, then to the door. It was obvious he was not sure what to do next. The pain in his head was so severe he could hardly think at all. With John inside and standing in front of him, he felt he had no further need to use Marsha as a shield. He pushed her aside, but kept his gun pointed at John.

Marsha moved across the room and knelt down on the floor beside Mary. She took hold of Mary's hand, more for her own support than for Mary's.

"Now what, Mike? What do we do now?"

John stood directly in front of Mike. He very slowly moved farther away from Mary and Marsha in order to keep them as much out of the line of fire as possible.

"Shut up! I have to think," Mike blurted out.

"As I see it, you don't have very many choices. You can give yourself up. If you do, I'll do all I can to see that you get help with those headaches. Or you can keep doing what you're doing and end up getting yourself shot, or worse end up in a very small cell in the basement of the state mental hospital where you'll never see the light of day again. What's it going to be?" John asked, trying to keep his voice as calm as possible under the circumstances.

"Stop moving around," Mike demanded.

John stopped and stood perfectly still. He could see Mike was trying to think, but with the pain it was difficult. John knew he had to get the gun away from Mike before he hurt someone.

"Mike, if you give yourself up to the police, I'll see to it you get help."

"You can't help me, no one can help me."

The tone of Mike's voice showed how deeply he was convinced that there was no help for him. He had come to the conclusion that this was the way it was always going to be. There was no help. Therefore, there was no hope.

"I can, and you know it."

Mike looked at John. He wondered if John meant what he was saying. It was difficult for him to comprehend the meaning of all that was going on. Mike began looking around the room, trying to think of what he should do. He was having difficulty understanding what was really going on around him, even though he was a part of it all.

Without realizing it, Mike let his hand, the one with the gun in it, slowly fall to his side. John took advantage of the opportunity. He quickly reached behind his back and pulled the gun from his belt. Raising it quickly, he pointed the gun directly at Mike's face and moved to within a few feet of him.

John's sudden movement and the sudden appearance of a gun startled Mike. He just stared at the gun for several seconds, then looked at John.

"Drop the gun, Mike."

John's voice was quiet and in control. He hoped Mike wouldn't force him to use the gun. Yet, John knew he could shoot Mike, if Mike gave him no other choice.

John took another step closer to Mike. Mike looked at John and began to grin. John had a feeling Mike was going to try to shoot him, even with a gun pointed right at him.

Without warning, John shot out a hard left jab. It caught Mike on the point of his chin, snapping his head back. It sent him reeling back on his heels.

Mike stumbled backwards, dropping the gun as he tried to regain his balance. He fell back against the wall and slid down onto the floor.

It took Mike a couple of seconds to recover from the blow. He looked at John as he rubbed his chin, then looked toward the gun. He started to roll toward it, but Marsha kicked it across the room, well out of Mike's reach.

Mike looked with hatred at Marsha. His eyes filled with anger. She had betrayed him just like Mary. There was also hatred in his eyes for John. He started to get up.

"Don't even think about getting up. Stay right where you are."

The threat in John's voice was clear. Even in Mike's confused mind, he understood. He had heard that tone in John's voice before. The few times he had challenged John in the past had proven to be unwise. He leaned back against the wall and watched as John moved toward Mary.

Keeping Mike in sight, John reached down to help Mary to her feet.

"You all right?"

"I am now."

She stood in front of him and put her arms around him, resting her head on his shoulder. She couldn't remember when she had felt so much relief.

John wrapped one arm around her and held her up against him for a minute. There was a flood of relief that passed through him, too. She was dirty from crawling on the floor and a little shaken, but she was safe.

Marsha moved around behind John. Still keeping the gun pointed toward Mike, John took his arm from around Mary and gently guided her around behind him. They backed toward the door. Marsha unlocked the door and opened it. She stepped outside and held it for Mary. Mary stepped outside, but stopped to wait for John.

"Go down the alley to the right," John instructed them.

Mary hesitated for just a second, then started down the alley with Marsha. She looked back to see if John was following, but didn't see him. She stopped, but Marsha grabbed her by the hand and pulled her down the alley.

Lieutenant Palmer and another officer ran down the alley to get them. When they got to the women, they grabbed them and pulled them close to the building.

"Where's John?" Lieutenant Palmer asked.

"He's still in there."

The tone of Mary's voice showed how worried she was. She couldn't contain the fear of what might happen if he didn't get out of there.

"Take them around the corner," Lieutenant Palmer instructed the other officer.

The officer took the women to the end of the alley while Lieutenant Palmer started toward the door. Just as he got to the back of the car, he saw John backing out the door. John still had the gun in his hand.

"Mike, I meant what I said. You give yourself up to the police, and I'll do all I can to get you the help you need."

"The police are already here, aren't they?" Mike asked. It was really more of a statement than a question.

"Yes. They're here. There's no way out. Give yourself up. I don't want to see you hurt."

"Move away from the door. We'll take over now," Lieutenant Palmer said to John in almost a whisper.

John glanced sideways and saw Lieutenant Palmer crouched down behind the car. John wasn't a policeman, and he had done all he could do. It was time for the police to take over and finish what had to be done.

John moved away from the door and around behind the car. As he passed Lieutenant Palmer, he handed him the gun. He said nothing for there was nothing more to be said. It was up to Mike now. He could give himself up, or not, it was his choice. John had a pretty good idea what Mike's choice would be.

John started to walk toward the end of the alley where Mary was waiting for him. As John walked away, he could hear the police trying to talk Mike into giving up.

When John reached the end of the alley, he heard the loud report of several pistol shots and the loud crack of a high-powered rifle, then silence.

CHAPTER SIXTEEN

MARY HEARD THE SHOTS just as John stepped in front of her. The sound startled her, causing her to flinch. She looked down the alley over John's shoulder, then up at John. It was suddenly very clear to her what had happened. She reached out, put her arms around John and laid her head on his shoulder. Tears of relief rolled down her cheeks. Deep inside she knew Mike Flanders would never cause them problems again.

John looked over Mary's head at Marsha. She was just standing there, her face pale and her eyes open wide. It was clear that she knew what had happened, too. Even with the way that Mike had treated her, she still loved him.

Lieutenant Palmer came toward them, his head hanging down as he walked. It was evident that Mike had decided that he would never go back to the state mental hospital. No one wanted it to end this way, least of all Lieutenant Palmer.

"I'm sorry. He gave us no choice," Lieutenant Palmer said as he walked up to Marsha.

Marsha just looked at him for a couple of seconds. As the tears began to run down her cheeks, she threw her hands over her face and cried. Lieutenant Palmer took her in his arms in a feeble attempt to comfort her.

The lieutenant looked at John as if he were looking for help. He didn't know what to say or do that would make everything all right. There were no words to comfort her.

John looked down the alley. He could see several police officers milling around near the car. An ambulance was pulling into the alley.

"Let's get out of here," John said softly to Mary.

Mary said nothing. She simply turned in his arms and let him lead her toward a police car. She leaned against him as they walked, her arm around him, his arm around her.

A young police officer opened the car door for them and they got in the backseat. Mary laid her head on John's shoulder and closed her eyes.

Lieutenant Palmer helped Marsha into another police car, then closed the door. He walked over to talk to John.

"Officer Michaels will take you where you want to go. I would appreciate it if the two of you would come down to the police station tomorrow and make your statements."

"Sure," John replied.

John wasn't interested in talking about it now anyway, and he was sure Mary felt the same way. He just wanted to take her away from here.

Lieutenant Palmer nodded, and Officer Michaels got into the car. After finding out where they wanted to go, Officer Michaels didn't say anything more as he drove them back to the cabin.

When they turned down the lane to the cabin, John noticed the sun was going down. It had been a long day.

Officer Michaels stopped the car. John helped Mary out of the car.

"Thank you," John said to Officer Michaels, then turned and led Mary toward the cabin.

"I'll stop by tomorrow to take you to headquarters to make your statements," Officer Michaels said.

"How about right after lunch? I'm sure Miss Weston is very tired."

Officer Michaels simply nodded his approval, then drove away as John and Mary went into the cabin.

MARY WAS STILL QUITE SHAKEN by the happenings of the day. It had been a long day and a frightening experience. She was tired.

John was almost certain she would be hungry, as they had not eaten since breakfast. He knew that he was hungry.

"Hungry?" John asked softly as he took her in his arms.

"A little," she replied as she wrapped her arms around him. She didn't want to let go of him, not just yet. It was such a relief to be back at the cabin with him.

"Why don't you take a warm shower and get into something comfortable. I'll fix us something to eat," he suggested.

Reluctant to leave the security of his arms, she looked up at him. The look in her eyes expressed her love for him. He kissed her lightly on the forehead, then let go of her. John watched her as she went into the bedroom. He went to the kitchen and prepared a light dinner.

As he made a couple of small salads he could hear the shower running in the other room. He had dinner ready and the table set before she was out of the shower. John sat down in a chair to wait for her. It gave him time to think.

Mary interrupted his thoughts as she entered the living room wearing his robe. She still looked rather tired, but better after her shower. She walked over and sat down on the arm of the chair. He put his arm around her waist.

"Feel better?"

"Much better. I think I'll have something to eat and go to bed. I'm really tired," she said as she took his hand in hers.

John stood up and helped her to her feet. They walked to the kitchen table and sat down. It was a simple dinner that provided for the needs of the body and satisfied their hunger.

When they had finished, they went into the bedroom. John helped her take her robe off. As he laid the robe over the chair in the corner, she climbed into the bed. She was wearing the top of his pajamas. He pulled the covers over her and kissed her on the forehead.

"I'm going to take a shower, then I'll come to bed."

Mary smiled up at him, but didn't reply. She snuggled down as he straightened the covers over her and kissed her again. He knew it wouldn't be long before she would be asleep.

John turned out the small light next to the bed and went into the bathroom. He took a long warm shower. It felt good to have the warm water run over him. After drying himself, he put on the bottoms of his pajamas.

Entering the bedroom, he found Mary sleeping. He paused just a minute to watch her. It seemed to him that she must feel safe and secure to sleep so peacefully after such a trying day.

He moved to the other side of the bed and carefully pulled back the covers, trying not to disturb her. He eased himself into the bed next to her and pulled the covers up.

As Mary rolled up against him, he put his arm under her so she could lay her head on his shoulder. She curled up against him, laying her arm across his chest. He laid quietly just thinking and watching her. Her breathing was that of someone who was almost asleep.

John was feeling very content and happy. He couldn't help but think that this was the way it should be.

"Will you marry me?" John whispered so softly that he could hardly be heard. It was more of a thought, than a question.

"Yes" she whispered and snuggled against him.

WHEN MORNING ARRIVED, it found the two lovers sleeping. They were wrapped in each other's arms. It wasn't until mid-morning that they decided to get up.

By the time noon came around they were dressed and ready to face the day. They had their lunch, then waited on the front porch for Officer Michaels to come and get them.

It was about five to one when Officer Michaels arrived. He drove them to the police station where they gave their statements of what had happened to Lieutenant Palmer.

When they were finished, Officer Michaels took John and Mary to Julie and Bill's home so John could get his car. They spent a couple of hours talking before Mary and John got into John's car and drove back to the cabin.

Mary and John spent the next four days enjoying themselves by laying on the bank of the river in the warm sun, doing a little swimming in the river and catching up on their lives over the past twenty years. They also spent some time discussing their future together.

A note of Interest: On the morning of September 23, 2009 a fire broke out in the Thompson Building. The fire almost destroyed the entire building, leaving the front façade standing. Since the façade was unstable, it has had to be supported until a decision of what to do with it is determined.
For more information on the Thompson Building and the historic district of Depot Town, you might want to contact the Ypsilanti Historical Society at www.ypsitantihistorcialsociety.org.

Made in the USA
Columbia, SC
08 January 2018